THE TALE of Angelino Brown

Also by David Almond

A Song for Ella Grey

The Boy Who Climbed into the Moon

The Boy Who Swam with Piranhas

Clay

Counting Stars

The Fire-Eaters

Half a Creature from the Sea: A Life in Stories

Harry Miller's Run

Heaven Eyes

Kit's Wilderness

Mouse Bird Snake Wolf

My Dad's a Birdman

My Name Is Mina

The Savage

Secret Heart

Skellig

Slog's Dad

The Tightrope Walkers

The True Tale of the Monster Billy Dean

THE TALE OF Angelino Brown

DAVID ALMOND

illustrated by
ALEX T. SMITH

WALKER
BOOKS

First published 2017 by Walker Books Ltd
87 Vauxhall Walk, London SE11 5HJ

2 4 6 8 10 9 7 5 3 1

Text © 2017 David Almond (UK) Ltd
Illustrations © 2017 Alex T. Smith

The right of David Almond and Alex T. Smith to be identified as author
and illustrator respectively of this work has been asserted by them in
accordance with the Copyright, Designs and Patents Act 1988

This book has been typeset in Sabon

Printed and bound in Great Britain by Clays Ltd, St Ives plc

British Library Cataloguing in Publication Data:
a catalogue record for this book is available from the British Library

ISBN 978-1-4063-5807-0

www.walker.co.uk

For Catherine Clarke
D.A.

For my art teacher, Pam Goodwin, for all
your inspiration and encouragement
A.T.S.

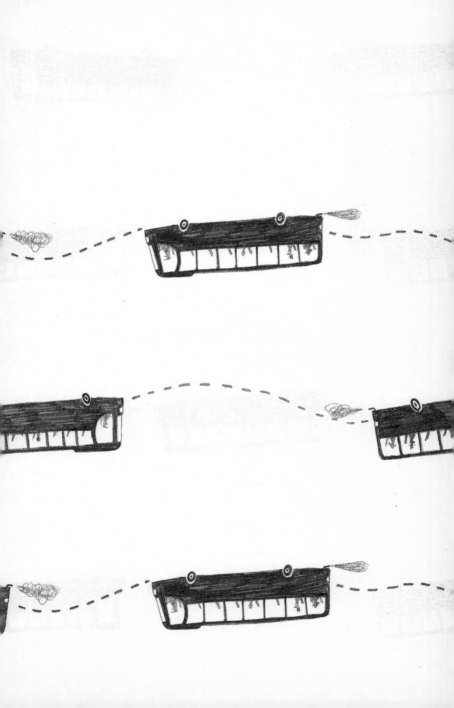

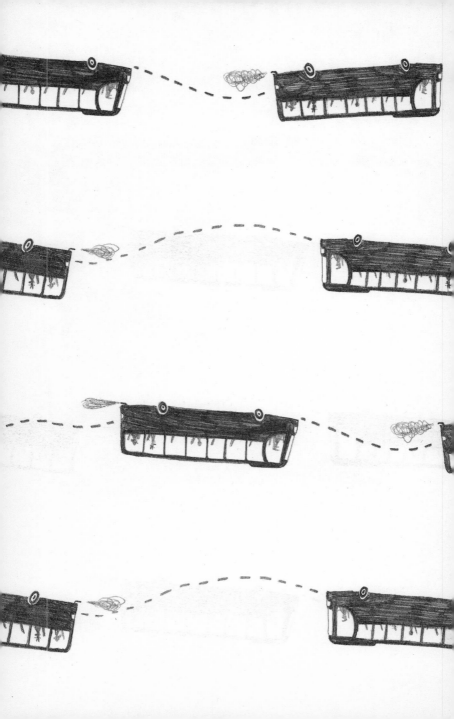

1

Here we go. All aboard. This is Bert, on his bus. He's been driving the same bus on the same road for ten long years. Ten years! That's longer than some of us have been alive! And for the ten years before that he drove another bus along another road on the other side of town. I know some folk would love to drive a bus. Mebbe you would. Mebbe Bert did when he started, way back in the distant days when he was young and bright and full of hope. But not now. Oh no, not now! Mr Bertram Brown has had quite enough. What a way to spend a life! Start stop start stop start stop start stop. Brakes sighing, doors creaking, engine throbbing. Traffic lights, traffic jams, hold-ups, roadworks, glaring sun, fog and puddles, ice and bloomin' snow.

And bus stops! What's the point of bus stops? All them people waiting, all them bloomin' hands held out. "Stop here, Bus Driver! Let us onto your cosy bus!" Passengers! Who invented passengers?

Old ladies with their sticks; smelly old blokes with their wobbly hands and dribbly gobs; dippy mothers with their screaming toddlers and babies puking in their arms. Wheelchairs and shopping bags and pushchairs and parcels. Lads with their lasses and lasses with their lads making lovey-dovey eyes and going *coo coo coo* and holding bloomin' hands.

And kids! Kids! Don't get Bert started about kids! Who on earth invented *them*? Cheeky snotty-nosed creatures. "Let us off with ten pence, Mister! I dropped me money in the gutter, Mister! I'm not fifteen, I'm only eight! Look out! Your back wheel's catching up with your front wheel! Stop the bus I want a wee-wee! Stop the bus I want a—" Kids! What's the point of them?

Oh heck, here he is at St Mungo's yet again. And here they come, the little brats. "One at a time! Keep in order! Sit down! Stop that giggling! Stop that screeching! Stop that racket!" Kids! Lock them up and chuck away the bloomin' key! Kids! "Shut up! Sit down! Sit *down*!"

At least it's nearly over. Bert's getting on. Look at him. Hardly any hair at all. It'll soon be time for retirement. Freedom at last! No more driving for old Bert. No more bus stops! No more passengers! No more kids! No more rotten cheeky kids!

But hang on... What's this? What's up? There's a fluttering in Bert's chest! He's gone all wibbly and wobbly and wiggly and waggly! His jacket's getting tighter. He can hardly breathe. His head's a-spinning. His heart's a-thumping, *bang bang bang! Bang bang bang!* Must be a heart attack! Bert's having a bloomin' heart attack!

He slams his foot down on the brake. The bus swivels to a stop where there's not a bus stop to be seen. "What's the problem, Bert?" the passengers yell. "There's no bus stop here. We've got homes to go to. We've got jobs to get to! The wheels on the bus don't go round and round and round..."

Get an ambulance! Bert wants to yell. But he cannot speak. And the fluttering's getting faster and his heart is banging harder and his jacket's getting tighter.

This is it! he thinks.

le turns off the engine. The passengers are yelling but he cannot hear a word.

Everything goes silent: beautifully, wonderfully silent.

So this is how it ends! thinks Bert. Bye-bye, sweet world!

But ... wait a sec. Yes, there's all that banging and fluttering and flickering around his chest. Yes, there's all that wibbling and wobbling in his head. But there's not a drop of pain. It's not a heart attack. It can't be. What a relief. Phew! So what *is* it, then? Oh! It's something in his chest pocket. It's something in there with the pens and the timetables. It's something moving. He reaches in, he fiddles around. Bloomin' heck. What's this little thing, jumping and fluttering about inside his jacket pocket?

He pulls it out. Lifts it up. It's alive!

It stands there on his hand. It's got wings. It's wearing a white dress thing. *It can't be...* Can it?

"What's that?"

A girl in a yellow jumper and yellow jeans appears. She's standing beside the driver's compartment, even though there's a sign right above her head that says:

IT IS FORBIDDEN
TO TALK TO OR OTHERWISE DISTRACT
THE ATTENTION OF THE DRIVER

"What is it?" she says.

Bert frowns.

"Nothin'," he says.

"It's not nothing. It's a—"

"Sit *down*!" he says.

He stares at the thing in his hand. It stares back at him. *It is!* It's a bloomin' angel.

He puts it back into his chest pocket.

"What's going on, Driver?" shouts somebody from the back of the bus.

"Little problem with the engine!" Bert calls. "Panic over!"

He switches the engine on again.

"What's his *name*?" says the girl.

"Whose name?"

"*His* name."

She points at Bert's pocket. The angel's moving about in there.

"Is he your little boy?" she says.

"I haven't *got* a little boy!" snaps Bert.

"You *have*! In *there*! In your *pocket*!"

"Sit down, you, or you'll be off my bus!"

The girl sits down but she keeps staring at Bert.

Bert feels the angel fluttering about beside his heart. At the first set of traffic lights he peeps into his pocket and sees two shiny little eyes peeping back at him.

"I'll take you home to Betty," Bert whispers. "She'll know what to do."

"Get a move on, Driver!" somebody shouts.

The lights have changed. Bert drives. He heads through the streets towards the depot. Passengers get on and off. He takes the fares, he gives the change. He doesn't moan. He says "please" and "thank you".

"What's up with him today?" somebody whispers.

"He's getting on," answers her friend. She taps her head and winks. "Losing his marbles," she says.

They giggle together.

"Poor old Bert," they say.

"I have to get off here," says the girl in yellow.

"Off you go, then," says Bert.

14

"Here's a midget gem," she says.

"A what?"

"For your little boy."

Bert glares at her. She laughs. A tiny hand is reaching upwards from his pocket. The girl puts the sweet into it. The hand and the sweet disappear. The girl laughs again.

"He's *lovely*!" she says.

"Off!" snaps Bert.

She gets off. She waves.

"See you again!" she calls. "Me name's Nancy Miller."

Bert drives on. His pocket is peaceful now. He peeps in and sees the angel licking the midget gem. It seems to be humming a little tune. Bert finds himself humming along with it.

At last the bus is nearly empty. Nearly at the journey's end. There's just one young bloke left, a bloke in black with a black moustache and black sunglasses.

He stands at the door, waiting to get off. Bert puts the brake on. The doors open.

"Last stop," says Bert.

The bloke doesn't move.

"End of the line, mate," says Bert.

"What you got in there?" says the bloke.

He points to Bert's pocket.

"Nothing," says Bert. "Off you go."

The bloke gets off, but he keeps on watching as the doors close and the bus moves away.

"Passengers!" mutters Bert.

He drives on.

The bloke takes a phone out of his pocket. He dials a number.

"It's me, Boss," he says. "I've just seen something we might be very interested in."

2

The bus is silent and empty. It's getting dark. Bert is still humming along with the little angel as he drives into the depot.

Some of the blokes have been waiting for him. They want him to come for a pint. They often go together to the Bus Driver's Arms to have a good moan about traffic jams and bus stops and passengers and bloomin' kids.

"No thanks, mates," says Bert. "Not tonight."

"What's up, Bert?" says his best mate, Sam.

"Nothin', Sam," says Bert.

The blokes watch him leave the depot.

"That's not like him," says Sam. "He's the best moaner of us all!"

Bert walks homeward. The sky's streaked with orange and red. Stars are shining in the darkest parts, just above the horizon. He walks through the park. The moon rises and shines down on him. Bert hesitates. He lifts the angel out of his pocket and lets it stand on his hand again. It shakes its wings and they shine and flicker in the moonlight. It looks just like an angel's supposed to look, just perfect.

"Who are you?" Bert whispers.

The angel stares back at Bert, like it hasn't a clue. It points to the pocket and starts to climb Bert's sleeve towards it. Bert helps the angel on its way, patting the pocket into place as the angel drops in again. He walks on, into Bus Conductor's Lane and through the gate to his little terraced house, Number 15.

"Hello, love!" calls Betty as he steps inside.

She comes to give him a kiss.

"Had a good day?" she says.

"Not bad," he says. "I found this, Betty."

He takes the angel out and puts it on the table next to a vase of chrysanthemums. It stands there looking up at them.

"It's an angel," says Betty.

"I know. It was in me pocket."

"How did it get in *there*?"

Bert shrugs. The angel licks its fingers.

"Dunno," Bert says.

"He's nice," says Betty.

"Is he?"

"Course he is. Look at him."

"Suppose he is," says Bert.

"Does he do anything?" says Betty.

"Like what?"

"Does he talk or something? Or fly or something?"

"Dunno. I've not known him very long. He hums a bit."

"Do you think he likes chips?"

"You could try him. He definitely likes midget gems."

"I'll do him an egg as well, eh?"

"Good idea."

Betty goes to the cooker to put the chip pan on.

"Do you think we should tell anybody?" she calls.

"Like who?"

"Like the police or something. Mebbe he's been reported missing."

"I'll look in the paper, eh?"

"Aye, there'll mebbe be something in there, Bert."

Bert sits down in his chair and opens the paper. It's all about wars and bombs, and the storms in the West Country that get worse every year, and kids looking for jobs that don't exist. The Prime Minister's wife has just bought a lovely frock in a charity shop and says that when people pull together they can overcome anything. A turtle has predicted the winner of the next World Cup. But a missing angel? Not a dicky bird. Bert shrugs. Mebbe something'll come up later on the telly.

He looks at the angel.

"Are ye all right?" says Bert.

The angel says nothing.

"Make yourself at home," Bert tells him.

The angel flutters his wings then sits down against the vase.

"Good lad," says Bert.

Then he drops the paper over his face and has a snooze. The angel rests his head on his knees and does nothing. Bert snores and the picture of the Prime Minister's wife flutters. The smell of cooking chips wafts through the house. Betty starts singing "Hernando's Hideaway" and thinks about when she and Bert were young and daft, when they were courting, and in love.

She fries three eggs and does a pan of beans. She puts the food on two big plates and one little saucer and carries them to the table. The angel gets one egg, three chips and seven beans. There's bread and butter as well, and two types of sauce, red and brown.

"Bert," she says. Bert rubs his eyes and the paper slides away from his face. He goes to the table and sees the angel looking down at a saucer of egg, beans and chips. Bert shakes his head.

"Thought it was a dream," he says. "But it's not, is it?"

"Come on, little'n," says Betty kindly. "Eat up."

She puts some beans on her fork and puts them in her mouth.

"Just like that," she says.

She picks up one of the angel's chips and pretends to fly it towards the angel's mouth.

"Open wide!" she says.

The angel just stares.

"You have to eat," she says. "Bert, tell him."

Bert chews a chip and swallows it to show the angel how it's done.

"You have to eat," he agrees. "Just like your..."
He hesitates.

"Ha! I nearly said 'like your mam and dad'."
Betty giggles.

"Come on," she says. She dips the tip of her little finger into the angel's baked beans. She holds it to the angel's lips. "Go on," she whispers. "Just a little lick."

"Put some sauce on it," says Bert.

She puts a tiny dab of tomato ketchup onto her finger as well. She holds it to the angel's mouth.

"Go on," she says. "Just for Betty."

And a tiny tongue comes out of the angel's mouth and licks Betty's finger. Betty gasps for joy.

"See?" she says. "It's easy! And isn't it tasty?

Now, how about a bit of this chip?"

In the end, the angel eats half a chip and four beans. He tries some egg but his face twists up and he spits it out again.

"I think he'd rather have some midget gems," says Bert.

They switch the telly on for the news. Library closed down to make way for a Daftco Express. More bombs and bullets in the Middle East and more floods in Bangladesh. Footballer won't play because he's got a bad back. There's a bit at the end about a celebrity eating a gorilla's toenail. Nothing about an angel. Ah, well.

Betty tells Bert she had a lovely day. She's the cook at St Mungo's.

"Sometimes," she says, "the bairns are just so lovely."

Bert grunts.

"I know!" says Betty. "Maybe he'd like to come to school!"

She smiles at the little angel.

"Would you like to go to school with me?" she says.

The angel blinks. He burps.

"Probably doesn't know what a school *is*, does he?" says Bert.

"No," says Betty. "But it'd do him good, Bert. Get him out to see a bit of the world. What do you think?"

Bert ponders.

"You're probably right," he says.

"And you could take him out on the bus one day."

"Aye, mebbe I could."

"The bairns at school'll love him."

She clears the table. She looks out of the kitchen window.

"What a lovely night!" she says. "Look at all them stars!"

The angel yawns.

"Poor thing," says Betty. "Been a long day, has it? Come on, let's get you to bed."

She fetches a cardboard box from the cupboard and lines it with cotton wool. She picks the angel up and lays him down in it. He shuffles a bit to get his wings comfortable. Betty puts a clean dishcloth over him to keep him warm.

"We should give him a name, Bert," she says.

"Angelino," says Bert.

"That's a good idea!"

Bert takes his bus driver's magic marker out of his pocket and writes the name on the side of the box:

ANGELINO

They look down at the angel. He looks back up at them. He farts.

"Angelino!" cries Betty.

"That'll be the beans," says Bert.

Angelino farts again.

"Bad Angelino!" says Betty.

Angelino giggles. Bert grins.

Betty reaches down and touches his little cheek.

"Get a good sleep and I'll take you to school tomorrow."

"Night-night, young'n," says Bert.

Angelino begins to snore, very softly.

"Ee, Bert," says Betty. "We've got our own little angel."

3

Bert and Betty sleep like babies.

Next morning, Bert puts on his bus driver's uniform. Betty puts on her cook's overall. She looks in the mirror to check she's clean and neat.

She pops into the other bedroom, where there's a single bed, and a photograph of a little boy hanging on the wall. She lifts the photograph down, as she does every morning, and kisses it, as she does every morning.

"Good morning, love," she whispers to it, as she does every morning.

Then she hangs the photograph up again, goes downstairs and tugs the living-room curtains open.

The sun's shining, nice and bright.

"Lovely!" she says to herself.

She goes to the table. There he is, fast asleep in his cardboard box.

"Rise and shine!" she says.

The little angel just turns over.

"Kids!" she says.

She laughs, and puts her hands into the box and gently lifts him out. He's so light it's like he's hardly there at all.

"Can't just lie there all day, you know," she whispers.

Bert comes down the stairs. "Little rascal!" he says.

They giggle as Angelino wakes up and rubs his eyes and looks at them.

"Peepo!" says Betty.

Angelino stares at her.

"Good *morning*, son!" she says.

"He's still in Dreamland, pet," says Bert.

Betty wets a tissue with some water then gently dabs his little face with it. Angelino wriggles and squirms and Betty smiles.

"Can't have you going to school with all that

sleepy in your eyes, can we?" she says. "There, all done! And you look lovely!"

Angelino has three cornflakes and a splash of milk and a tiny bit of Bert's bacon sandwich for his breakfast.

"Good lad," says Bert.

"You've got to grow up healthy and strong for us," says Betty.

They gaze at him for a while.

Angelino gazes back.

They go on gazing for a long, long time.

"Whoops!" says Bert at last. "Time to go! There's a bus to drive and passengers and bus stops and tons of bloomin' kids."

Betty polishes his bus driver's badge with her handkerchief, as she does every morning. She tells him not to be so grumpy with the passengers, as she does every morning.

"Me? Grumpy?" Bert says, as he does every morning.

He kisses her on the cheek.

"Bye-bye, pet. Bye-bye, little'n."

"Bye-bye, Bert," says Betty.

She lifts Angelino's hand and waves with it.

"Say 'Bye-bye, Bert'," she tells the angel.

She laughs.

"He didn't say it but I know he means it. Bye-bye, lovely Bert."

Bert strides down the path in the sunshine. He turns back at the gate – and just look at him.

There's a big grin on Bert's face.

Angelino is waving, all by himself.

4

Now Betty's walking through the streets towards St Mungo's School. She passes Sally Simpkin's Sweet Shop and the Particularly Perfect Pie Shop. She's carrying her red flowery shopping bag. People wave at her through windows and doorways and she pauses and has a natter with them about the weather or the Prime Minister's wife or those dreadful wars that are happening all around the world.

Betty's very popular and they're all nice friendly folk, as most folk are.

"She did look pretty in that frock," they say, and "What on earth'll we do when the sea gets as high as the bedroom windows?" and "Why can't they just *stop* their silly bombing? That's what I want to know!"

Betty's particular friend is Doreen McTavish, who runs the coffee shop in Blister Square. They sit down together at the little table outside it, under an apple tree, and share a pot of coffee and a toasted teacake.

"I've got something to show you," says Betty. "Close your eyes."

Doreen closes her eyes. Betty opens her shopping bag and lifts out Angelino and places him on the table. Angelino blinks in the sunlight and puts his hands behind his back and stares up at Doreen.

"Open up," says Betty.

Doreen looks. She blinks. She goggles.

"It's an angel!" she says at last.

"I know," says Betty.

"Where did you get it?"

"Bert found him," says Betty. "In his pocket."

"In his *pocket*?"

"Aye. When he was driving the bus."

"Ee, wonders never cease."

"He's called Angelino."

"That's a nice name," says Doreen. "Very pleased to meet you, lad."

She puts her hand out as if to shake Angelino's hand. The little angel just looks at it.

"He doesn't speak," explains Betty. "Or we don't think he does. This is my friend Doreen, Angelino."

Doreen nibbles the teacake.

"I saw an angel once," she says.

"Did you?"

"Well, a statue of one, but very lifelike. In the church. I think he's still in there. He's got a spear and he's killing some kind of horrible monster."

Betty frowns.

"I don't think our Angelino gets up to that kind of thing. Do you, pet?"

Angelino stares up at her.

"Do you kill horrible monsters, Angelino?" says Doreen.

Betty laughs.

"The very idea!" she says. "Give him a raisin, Betty. He seems to have a sweet tooth."

Doreen puts a raisin on her fingertip and lets Angelino lick it off. She giggles at the feeling of the angel's little tongue.

"You're very lucky, Betty," she says. "What does Bert think?"

"Bert? He thinks he's nice."

"That's nice."

They both gaze at Angelino.

Doreen leans across and kisses her friend's cheek.

"I'm so happy for you both," she says.

Then she starts telling Betty about her daughter who's backpacking in Australia and her son who's put a new electric fence around his house in Kent. They sigh and close their eyes and let the lovely sunlight fall on them. Angelino spreads his wings and leans back against a milk jug.

"The only bad thing he seems to do is to let fly occasionally," says Betty.

"Let fly?"

"You know. Fart."

"Well, that's nothing, is it? Not in the great scheme of things."

After she's said goodbye to Doreen, Betty carries Angelino in the shopping bag towards school. They have to pass St Mungo's Church. Betty hesitates.

"I wonder..." she murmurs to herself.

She goes inside.

There's just one old lady kneeling in the front row saying her prayers to a statue of Jesus. Candles are burning under another statue, one of some saint with an arrow in his leg.

Betty lifts Angelino out of the bag. She lets him stand on her hand. He looks around as if there's nothing special about the place. Betty carries him over to the statue that Doreen was talking about. True enough, this angel's massive and he's got a great big spear in his hand. There's an ugly snake squirming under his feet and you can see that the angel's furious and is just about to kill it.

Betty holds Angelino up high so he can see the angel and its wings.

"That's an angel too," she says. "Just like you are."

But there's hardly any similarity at all. Angelino's far too small and gentle. He farts, and the sound of it echoes through the nearly empty church.

"Little devil!" whispers Betty.

She hears footsteps and tucks Angelino back into the bag. She finds a priest at her side. It's Father Coogan from Connemara.

"Good morning," he says. "Mrs Brown, isn't it?"

"Betty."

"May I be of help, Betty?"

"I was just admiring your angel."

"Ha! A splendid specimen, don't you think?"

"Oh, he's lovely. Very grand. Are all angels like that?"

The priest stares at the statue of the angel as if he's never seen it before.

"Who can tell?" he says. "It's said they come in many forms. The Devil himself was said to have been an angel, way, way back."

"The Devil himself?"

"Yes, Betty." The priest tugs at the white collar around his neck. He lowers his voice. "To be honest, Betty, we aren't really believing in things like angels and monsters. Not these days."

"Really?"

"Yes, really. We're more into the modern type of thing."

"The modern type of thing?"

"Yes, Betty. Like getting the guitars out, and the church website, that kind of thing."

A farting noise comes from the shopping bag.

Betty coughs. Father Coogan frowns, then shrugs.

"Well, I could stand here nattering all day," he says, "but parish business calls, I'm afraid."

"That's OK."

"Would you like me to pray for you, Betty?"

"Pray for what?"

"For your health," he says. "Your contentment. Your happiness."

She laughs.

"What an idea!" she says. "I'm fit as a flea, content as a cow and happy as a horse!"

"Excellent!" he says. "Then I'll say farewell."

"That was the priest," Betty whispers to the shopping bag when he has left. "He's Father Coogan from Connemara."

The lady praying to Jesus turns round to stare at her.

Betty smiles and waves.

The lady turns back and prays louder and faster.

Betty goes out into the sunshine and continues her walk to school.

Bert passes by, driving his bus. Betty waves and points down to the shopping bag. Bert waves back and toots the bus's horn three times.

"What a bloke!" Betty says to the shopping bag. "I've never known him do *that* before!"

She giggles, and wanders on past the War

Memorial and the Green Man pub. She doesn't see the skinny bloke in the black suit and the sunglasses standing in the dark alleyway next to Boggins, Best Of Butchers. Hang on. Is that the bloke who was the last to get off Bert's bus last night? Yes, it's the same bloke. And he's watching. And he's writing something down in a notebook. And he's taking a phone out of his pocket, and he's making a call.

5

Imagine this. You're in your school yard at play-time and somebody yells, "Come and have a look at *this*!"

So you run with everybody else to the school kitchen window. And you look in and you see an angel sitting on a shelf while the cook stirs the gravy and whisks the custard and mashes the spuds. You might think he's just a little ornament. You might think he's a little doll that the cook's brought in with her. But then you see him walking back and forth on the shelf. You see him leaning over the custard to smell it, and then the cook puts a tiny bit on her finger and lets him lick it, and she does the same with the gravy and he twists his face and spits it out.

What do you do? You goggle and gape and gasp with everybody else. You don't believe your own eyes but you have to. It's real.

There's an angel, licking custard, in the school kitchen!

That's what happens in the yard at St Mungo's School that morning. Everybody runs to the window. Betty waves at all the faces. She holds little Angelino up so everybody can see him. The small kids squeeze past the big kids to get a better view. Angelino stares back at all those goggling eyes.

Then somebody cries out in delight. "That's Bert Brown's little boy!"

It's Nancy Miller, the girl from the bus.

"I saw him yesterday!" she says. "I gave him a midget gem! Hello! Hello, little angel!" She pushes her face right against the window. "Hello!"

Does he recognize her? Yes, he does! He stares for a few seconds, then he lifts his hand and waves, just like he did to Bert. Nancy can't contain herself. She does a little skip, a little dance, a little—

"Now then, children, what is going on here?"

It's Mrs Mole, the Acting Head Teacher. She's a stocky, round-faced lady with round steel spectacles and a green overcoat. She's standing in for the Real Head Teacher, Mr Donkin, who has been off school with his nerves since the last School Inspection.

"It's an angel, *señorita*!" cries a small, dark-haired boy wearing a Barcelona strip and orange football boots.

"Don't fantasize, Jack Fox. Step aside, children, and let me see."

The children step aside. Mrs Mole comes to the window. She looks hard at Angelino. He looks back at her.

She polishes her spectacles, puts them back on and looks again.

She closes her eyes, opens them and looks again.

"It's an angel," she says.

"Yes, Miss," says Nancy.

"How did it get here?"

"Betty brought him, Miss!" says Nancy. "I seen him yesterday and—"

"It is *Mrs Brown* to you," says Mrs Mole. "And it is *saw* not *seen*. And..."

She pauses. What should an Acting Head Teacher do in such circumstances?

"And you must all disperse to your classrooms *right now,* and I shall ... investigate."

Nobody moves.

She takes off her spectacles and glares.

"Disperse!" she says in a Very Stern and Head Teacherly voice. And they disperse, while she heads for the kitchen to speak to Betty.

6

"Bert found him, Miss," says Betty when Mrs Mole arrives in the kitchen.

"*Found* him?"

"In his pocket. On the bus."

Betty's trembling slightly – she's rather nervous in the company of the Acting Head Teacher.

"And is your husband used to finding such things?"

"Oh no, Miss. It's usually umbrellas. And gloves. And once somebody forgot a false leg…"

Betty bites her lip. Mrs Mole is staring down at Angelino, who is now on the worktop. Angelino grips the handle of a custard jug and leans right back so that he can return the gaze of the Acting Head Teacher. There's a drop of custard on his lip. He licks it off.

"And *what*," says Mrs Mole to little Angelino, "do *you* have to say about yourself?"

"Oh, nothing," says Betty nervously. "He can't talk, Miss."

"Can't talk?"

"No, Miss."

"Are you certain?"

"No, Miss."

"And what else cannot he do?"

"We don't know, Miss. But he likes eating custard and midget gems."

Mrs Mole flinches.

"Speak up," she says to Angelino. "I repeat, what do you have to say? Where are you from? What is your name?"

"He's called Angelino," says Betty.

"Angelino? How do you know?"

"We wrote it on his box."

"On his *box*?"

"Yes, Miss. With Bert's magic marker. *Angelino*."

Mrs Mole casts her eye around the kitchen. She frowns. There is nothing in the Acting Head Teacher's manual that has prepared her for this.

"I shall take some time to contemplate the matter," she says. "In the meantime, there is a school lunch to prepare, and we have a creature who has much to learn about himself and his world. He must attend lessons."

"Angelino?" says Betty.

"Yes, if that really is his name."

"But he's just—"

"He *looks* like a child: a child who has much to learn. And as our Secretary of State for Education, Mr Narcissus Spleen, so rightly said, any child who is not in a classroom is a child who is not learning. He will spend the rest of the morning with 5K studying English with Professor Smellie."

She takes a deep breath. She is very pleased with herself. Yes, this is how an Acting Head Teacher should behave.

"Bring Nancy Miller," she says. "She claims to know this silly thing. She can take the angel to the Professor."

7

Professor Smellie is a Very Clever Man. He is on secondment to St Mungo's from the University of Blithering-on-the-Fen. He is helping the school to Improve. He works with Clever Children to make them even cleverer so that they can attend his university and become cleverer still and then become Professors like him and teach the children of the future to become Professors themselves.

He has red curly hair, a crumpled black suit and a rather puzzled expression, as if he has lost something, or as if he can sense a deep dark hole somewhere near by. Right now, he is staring at the ceiling. The class is silent. The Professor is talking slowly and clearly. He doesn't notice Nancy slipping in through the door with Angelino standing on her outstretched palm.

"Beyond the simple sentence," he says, "is the compound sentence. This is where two clauses are joined together using a *connective*."

He turns his eyes to the class.

"Who," he enquires, "can tell me what a connective is?"

"It's the angel, *señor*!" calls out Jack Fox.

"The *what*?" demands the Professor.

Then he sees Nancy standing shyly there. He flinches, he blinks.

"You're late, girl," he says.

"Mrs Mole sent for me, sir," says Nancy. "I was told to bring Angelino to you, sir."

He looks at the thing standing on Nancy's hand. His face becomes even more puzzled than usual. The eyes of the children all shine with delight.

The Professor approaches. He stares. He closes his eyes tight then opens them again. Yes, the thing is still there, looking back at him.

"It's an angel, sir," says Nancy.

She wipes a drop of custard from Angelino's cheek.

"Mrs Mole says he has to learn, sir."

"Sensible woman," says the Professor. "Find it a seat."

"He's rather little for that, sir," says Nancy.

The Professor seems bemused by the problem.

46

"He could sit on my desk, sir," suggests Nancy. "There's plenty of room for him, sir."

"This is true. Sit him there, girl, and let us get on."

Angelino does a little skip and a dance as Nancy places him on her desk.

"Enough tomfoolery," declares the Professor. "We must concentrate. Time wasted in the classroom can never be recovered. I was explaining about connectives. Listen closely. There are simple connectives such as *but* and *so* and *and*." He stares at the ceiling again. "But there is also a broader and more complex range of possibilities. *Alternatively. Consequently. Therefore. Otherwise...*"

He continues with his list. The children of 5K grin and wave at Angelino. He grins and waves back. He farts and the children try to stifle their giggles.

"That'll be the custard," whispers Nancy.

"So," demands the Professor suddenly, "can anyone give me a sentence which contains an interesting and relevant connective?"

Jack Fox raises his hand.

"*Si, señor!*" he calls.

The Professor flinches.

"Why are you speaking Spanish, boy?" he snaps.

Jack rests his hand on the badge of his Barcelona strip.

"Because I am Lionel Messi, *señor!*" he announces.

He turns around to show the name and number printed on his back.

MESSI
10

The Professor groans.

"This is my sentence," Jack says. *"I am starving, consequently I cannot wait to get stuck into me dinner."*

"Technically correct," says the Professor. "However, *starving* is hyperbole, *stuck into* is slang, *cannot wait* is hyperbole again, it is *lunch* not *dinner*, and it is *my lunch* not *me lunch*. Anyone else? You?"

He points to Angelino.

"Come along," he says. "Give me a sentence which contains a complex and relevant connective."

Angelino leans on Nancy's pencil case. He stares back at the Professor.

"Try," says the Professor. "Do you think I have achieved what I have achieved without trying? Speak up!"

Angelino farts again.

Nancy grins at him.

"Can you speak?" she whispers into his little ear.

He climbs over Nancy's book and up her sleeve, perches on her collar and leans close to her ear.

And he whispers back to her. Yes, Angelino speaks.

"I don't know nowt," he says in a tiny voice.

Nancy gasps. She takes Angelino in her hand and looks at him in wonder.

"So?" demands the Professor. "What is his sentence?"

"He said 'I don't know nowt'!"

"*I don't know nowt?*" repeats the Professor. "Grammatically incorrect! Double negative! And it's *nothing*, not *nowt*! It should be 'I know nothing'. And where, may I ask, is the connective?"

"There isn't one, sir," says Nancy.

"Indeed there is *not*!"

The Professor turns away in exasperation.

"Who can help? Who can give the class a sentence that begins with 'I know nothing', continues with a complex connective and concludes with a second clause?"

Alice Obi raises her hand.

"*I know nothing,*" she says, "*therefore I must find out.*"

"Excellent!" says the Professor. "It is no surprise that you are one of my Gifted and Talented group."

Alice smiles sweetly. Nancy continues to stare at Angelino in awe. The Professor stares suspiciously into the void.

"Writing!" he says. "It is time for the writing task! Take out your books and pens and each write five sentences formed of two clauses joined by complex connectives. Begin now."

The class obediently prepare to do the task. The Professor sits down at the teacher's desk.

"Do not forget the date," he says. "And correct punctuation of course, and best handwriting, and each sentence should be numbered, and..."

His voice falters. His eyes focus in puzzlement on Angelino once more. Angelino waves. The Professor flinches.

Nancy gives the angel a pencil and a sheet of paper. He holds the pencil between two hands.

"Just do your best," Nancy whispers.

She helps to guide his pencil across the paper. He makes some marks.

"That's *brilliant*," she says.

Angelino looks at the other children writing. He flutters his wings.

"Write what you said," Nancy whispers.

She takes her hand away from his.

"Go on, Angelino. Give it a try."

Angelino flutters his wings again. And he writes. Yes, he writes. The pencil moves across the paper and he scrawls untidily:

ay doant no nowt

"That's fantastic, Angelino!" gasps Nancy. She herself writes:

An angel has whispered to me, therefore I am very pleased.

Angelino grins. He holds the pencil up straight and leans on it. The children continue with their task. Angelino watches the Professor and the Professor watches Angelino. Strange, the angel seems a little taller now. The minutes pass. Lunchtime approaches. The children's pens move across the pages, making words and sentences where before there was just empty space.

"Time!" announces the Professor.

He gathers in the children's books. He beams

at Alice Obi and murmurs, "Excellent." He takes Jack's work without giving it a glance. He edges towards Nancy and Angelino. He sees Angelino's sheet while taking Nancy's book.

He lifts the paper towards his eyes. He groans.

"No grammatical improvement at all!" he says. "What a disgraceful mess! Where is the capital letter? And the apostrophe? The silent *k*? Silent *w*? And it is *I* not *ay*. And where is the full stop? Does he know anything?"

"I don't know, sir," says Nancy.

"What *do* you know?" he asks Angelino.

Angelino says nothing.

"Where are you from?" says the Professor. "Who on earth are you?"

Angelino ponders, then climbs to Nancy's ear again.

"I don't know who I am," he whispers.

"*Well?*" demands the Professor.

"He said," says Nancy, "'I don't know who I am.'"

"I don't know who I *am*?" says the Professor. "How can anybody not know who he is?" His eyes light up. "But ah! You used the word *know* again.

Did you hear the *k* in it? Of course you didn't, because it is silent. The silent letter is one of the mysteries and joys of the English language. It is a letter that is not pronounced and so cannot be heard even though it is there. There are of course other words that begin with a *k* that cannot be heard." He looks around the class. "Examples?"

Jack Fox raises his hand.

"Sausage," he says.

"*Sausage?*" says the Professor. "Are you *mad*? You think there is a silent *k* in *sausage*?"

He stares at the void, picks up his briefcase, heads for the door.

"Well, *I* can't hear it," mutters Jack, as he jumps from his seat, feints, dodges and lashes an invisible ball into an invisible net.

8

Carrots, ketchup and custard, of course. There are many things in Betty's delicious school dinners that appeal to an angel with a sweet tooth. Angelino happily nibbles and licks. He turns up his nose at gravy and meat. He sits at a table with Nancy and her pals. They feed him with their fingertips and with their spoons. They ask him to speak, to say his name, to write, to dance, to fly.

"Slow down!" says Nancy. "How would you like it if you were a tiny angel on his first day in school?"

"You're right," says Jack. "Give him time to settle in."

So they're quiet, and they gaze at Angelino in amazement. When Betty's finished serving, she comes and sits with them. Angelino waves and does a little dance and climbs onto her arm.

"He did a *lesson*," says Nancy. "With the *Professor*!"

"With the *Professor*!" says Betty proudly. "Well, Angelino, I *am* impressed. Just wait till I tell Bert!"

"And Betty," says Nancy, "you'll never guess what. He spoke!"

Betty goggles and claps her hand across her mouth.

"Angelino! And what did he *say*?"

"Go on, Angelino," prompts Nancy. "Tell Betty what you said."

Angelino frowns. He farts. Nancy whispers in his ear.

He steps down from Betty's arm. He stands up straight, holds his hands behind his back, takes a deep breath, and says in a clear tiny voice, "I don't know nowt and I don't know who I am."

"Angelino!" cries Betty. "What a lovely voice you have!"

Angelino beams.

He says it again, louder this time.

"I don't know nowt and I don't know who I am!"

"Just wait till Bert hears *that*!" says Betty.

"And Angelino," says Jack, "it's a proper compound sentence!"

Betty's eyes shine with tears of joy. She takes the

angel in her hand and holds him high. She laughs.

"You're getting bigger and taller and heavier. I'm sure of it! Oh, what a lovely angel you're going to be."

"Sit down! Calm down!" It's the voice of Mrs Mole, who is patrolling the dining hall and trying to keep kids away from Angelino's table. "Control yourselves!"

She stamps her foot.

"We are trying to emerge from Special Measures and you are behaving like little *monsters*!" she cries. Her voice gets louder and screechier. How can she *cope* with all of this? Special Measures! Excited kids! And now an *angel* in their midst! "What," she screeches, "if another *School Inspector* turns up at our door?"

"Poor Mrs Mole," whispers Betty to Angelino. "She gets herself into such a tizz."

Mrs Mole comes over to Angelino's table.

"*You* are attracting far too much attention," she says.

Angelino sticks out his bottom and farts.

"That is *quite* enough of *that*!" says Mrs Mole.

Angelino stops and stares at her.

"I expect far better manners from an *angel*," she says.

"He's sorry, Miss," says Betty.

"I hope he is, Mrs Brown. It is *he* who should be showing an example to his fellow pupils."

"He will, Miss," promises Betty, in a rather trembly voice.

Mrs Mole leans down over Angelino.

"I shall," she says, "be keeping a very close eye on you, my boy."

And she wheels away.

"Oh, *Angelino*!" says Betty. "I'm so proud of you!"

She gives him a little kiss.

"Go on," she says. "Go off and play with your friends."

Mrs Mole isn't the only one who's keeping a close eye on our little angel this lunchtime. Beyond the school gates and across the road on the other side of the little park beyond stands a bloke in black. Yes, the same bloke as before. Strange, he looks quite a young bloke behind the shades and the moustache and the black, black suit. No more than a lad, really. He has a small pair of binoculars trained on Angelino. He has the notebook in his hand. And he has a phone to his cheek, and he's speaking into it.

"Yes, Boss," he says. "I've got him in me sights, Boss... No, I've not seen nowt like him never before, Boss. Never in me life, Boss... Yes, Boss, there'll be a way of making money from it. Yes, Boss, the circus mebbe. Or how about a church, Boss? A church'd give a lot of loot to get its hands on a proper real-life angel."

He goes on watching. He sees Angelino carried out into the school yard by Nancy. He sees all the excited kids gather around. And then a group of them break away and start a football game.

It's rough and tough and fast. A bunch of lads and lasses scampering around kicking and heading and yelling.

"To me!" call the kids. "On me head! Great shot! Bad luck! That's a foul! Red card, ref! What a goaaaaal! What a save! To me! To me! *Ouch!* To him! Bring him down! Get stuck in! Get stuck *in*!"

Jack Fox is the cleverest and quickest. He's the star. He runs like Lionel Messi, swerves like Lionel Messi, scores like Lionel Messi. In his imagination he *is* Lionel Messi. He laughs and grins and yells encouragement to the others.

"*Si!*" he calls. "*Maravilloso! Fantastico! Gol! Goooooool!*"

Angelino dances on Nancy's hand. He squeaks with delight. He runs around on her palm as if he's running around with the kids in the game. He swings his leg as if he's kicking the ball. He jumps up as if he's heading it. He jumps and jumps and then, oh goodness gracious...

"Boss!" gasps the bloke in black into his phone. "He's flying!"

9

Not very far. Not very high. But he does. He flies. He jumps off Nancy's hand into the air and hovers there for a few moments, a little bit higher than her head. And then down he tumbles, to the ground at Nancy's feet.

"Angelino!" she gasps in fright.

She's sure he must have broken something – a leg, a wing, an arm, his back, his skull. But he jumps to his feet. He giggles and gasps. He flaps his wings. He leaps back into Nancy's hands. He jumps again and flies again. A bit further. A bit higher. He lands back on her hands and gets ready to do it a third time. It's amazing. He seems to have grown yet again. Nancy has to use both hands to hold him. Then the football flashes past and he jumps towards it and nearly touches it.

Down to Nancy's hands again.

The ball flies past again and this time Angelino's after it. He flaps his wings so fast they can hardly be seen. And he catches the ball and wraps his arms around it and down they fall together to the ground.

"*Caramba!*" yells Jack Fox. "What a save!"

Angelino totters to his feet, the ball at his side. It's bigger than he is.

"You're on our team!" yells Jack. "Angelino, you're goalie! *El portero!*"

He carries the angel to where the goal is.

"You've got to stop the ball from going into that. *Comprende?*"

Angelino stares at Jack like he really, really wants to understand.

Jack shows him how it's done.

"Take a penalty," he says to Louis Lepp. "Just watch, Angelino!"

Louis puts the ball on the spot and takes a penalty kick. Jack dives to his left and catches the ball. He knocks a second penalty away with his fist.

"Get the idea?" he says to Angelino. "Now it's you."

He sets Angelino down between the posts. It looks hopeless. The angel's surely far too small to be defending such a space.

But his good pal Nancy believes in him.

"You can do it, Angelino!" she shouts.

Angelino narrows his eyes and stares at the ball. He flexes his knees just like a proper goalie.

"Not too hard!" shouts Louis Lepp.

Jack chips the ball. It swerves towards the corner of the goal. And look how Angelino leaps and flies and catches it, then spins through the air with the ball in his arms and comes back down to earth!

Everybody cheers.

"What a goalie! What a save!"

And that's how lunchtime passes by. The football game is huge. Everybody joins in. Nobody's bothered about winning or losing. They just want to see the brave angelic goalie flying through the air to stop the ball. He doesn't save it every time. Sometimes he catches the ball but can't stop it, and ball and angel fly together into the net. But what a treat it is! Nobody's ever seen anything like it. When the bell goes for the end of lunchtime, Angelino's skin is scuffed with mud and grass stains. His dress is all dishevelled and his eyes are shining bright. Jack carries him back into the school as if he's a hero, as if he's just won the European Cup. Dozens of kids flock after him, cheering and chanting his name.

"Angelino! Angelino! Angelino!"

"Jack *Fox*! Put that angel *down*!"

Mrs Mole, of course.

"And line up *properly*!" she snaps. "And stop that silly *noise*!"

Jack puts Angelino down by Nancy's side.

Strange, thinks Nancy. He's higher than my ankle now. I'm sure he wasn't so tall an hour ago.

"No *wonder*," cries Mrs Mole, "that Mr Donkin

64

has such trouble with his *nerves*!"

She is trying hard to be Very Stern, but her voice is wobbly. How can she cope with all this? She's just an ordinary little woman. But then she clenches her fists and forces herself to be a proper Acting Head Teacher.

"And no *wonder*," she snaps, "that this school is in such dire straits! Stand straight! Lips shut!"

"Must be the custard helping him grow," muses Nancy.

She reaches down. Angelino reaches up. They take each other's hand.

Just yesterday, thinks Nancy, he was little enough to fit into a bus driver's pocket.

"This is an educational *establishment*!" says Mrs Mole. "Not a *zoo* in which you run *amuck*!"

Nancy licks her finger. She dabs away a spot of mud from the angel's brow.

"You are here to be trained, to be *educated*, to be... What on earth are you *doing*, Nancy Miller?"

Nancy blinks.

"Wiping Angelino's brow, Miss."

"Wiping Angelino's brow? Wiping Angelino's *brow*! And what gives you the right, may I ask, to wipe an angel's brow when a teacher – particularly an Acting Head Teacher such as myself – is speaking?"

"I don't know, Miss."

"You don't *know*! Do you think you would find a pupil such as Alice Obi wiping an angel's brow when a teacher is speaking?"

"I don't know, Miss."

"Then I shall tell you. No, you would *not* find a Gifted and Talented pupil such as Alice Obi wiping an angel's brow when a teacher is speaking! You would *not* find a Gifted and Talented pupil allowing herself to be distracted by fripperies with wings and dresses and running amuck during a school lunchtime! Would you, Alice?

Alice, where *are* you?"

"I'm here, Mrs Mole," comes a voice.

"Step forward, Alice."

Alice steps out of the line. She has a book in her hand.

"Bring some sanity to this place," says Mrs Mole. "Tell us what *you* were doing this lunchtime."

"I was in the library, Mrs Mole."

Mrs Mole sighs with delight.

"And *that*," she says, "is how to spend your time instead of wasting it all on football and fripperies. Thank you, Alice. My faith in human nature – at least in that part of it represented by our Gifted and Talented pupils – is restored. And now *silence*! Line *up*!"

Nancy ponders Angelino. She can't restrain herself. She raises her hand.

"Please, Miss," she says.

Mrs Mole glares.

"Well?"

"Please, Miss," says Nancy. "Do you know if angels grow?"

Mrs Mole stamps her foot.

"What kind of question is *that*? DO I KNOW IF ANGELS *GROW*? Are you *mad*?"

"Do they, Miss?"

Red-faced Mrs Mole is about to yell some more, then Alice steps out of line again. She holds up her book. It's an ancient battered-looking thing.

"No," Alice says. "It seems they do not. I read it in here. It says that angels are always the same size.

They aren't born and they don't die. They are perfect beings that have always existed and will always exist."

Everybody looks at Angelino. He grins and waves back. He looks far from perfect. He leans against Nancy's leg.

"Maybe he's a very strange kind of angel," says Alice.

Mrs Mole groans. How can she *cope* with all of this?

"To your classes!" she commands.

"*Are* you a strange kind, Angelino?" asks Alice.

"I don't know nowt," he replies.

10

"Yes, Boss," says the bloke in black. "I seen it with me own eyes. Flyin' and playin' football, Boss... Yes, Boss. Definitely... No, Boss, can't see nowt now, Boss. They've gone inside, Boss."

"It's *saw* not *seen*," says the Boss. "It's *nothin'* not *nowt*. And it ain't your job to see nowt. It's your job to see everythin'. Get inside that school, K."

"It's got a fence around it, Boss. They won't let me in, Boss."

"Course they'll let you in. Tell them you're a School Inspector. Tell them you were passin' by and decided to drop in to give them a quick once-over."

"But they won't believe it," says the bloke in black. "I'm just a lad!"

"Then grow up fast! Take the shades off. Brush your hair. Stick your chest out. You're a Master of Disguise, aren't you?"

The bloke touches his shades, his moustache, his black hair, black suit, black tie. Master of Disguise.

Yes. That's what he's always been good at, ever since he was a little lad.

"Yes, Boss."

"So you can do it. Walk tall. Take the notebook. Make notes. Talk in a Deep and Confident voice, and watch your grammar when you speak."

The bloke in black takes a deep breath.

"But what does a School Inspector *do*, Boss?"

"He inspects, of course. He writes things down. He says what's wrong. He tells the teachers things'd better change or there'll be deep, deep trouble. He shows that he is in *command*. Now get in there and *do* it."

"OK, Boss," says the bloke.

"Be brave, K," says the Boss. "This is the moment you grow up and become a man."

"Is it, Boss?"

"Yes. Be Brave. Be Distinguished. And get that angel in your sights."

The bloke in black spits on his fingers and smooths down his hair. He takes off the shades, puffs out his chest, holds the notebook under his arm and sets off across the park towards the school.

He presses the bell by the school gates.

"May I help you?" says Samantha Cludd, the School Secretary, through the intercom.

"Indeed you may," says the bloke in black in a very deep voice. "I am a School Inspector."

"A School Inspector!" gasps Samantha Cludd.

"Yes," replies the bloke in black. "I was passing by and thought I would drop in to give you a quick once-over."

Samantha gasps again. Then there is silence. Then the voice of Mrs Mole comes through the intercom.

"How may I help you, sir?" she says.

"I am a School Inspector," repeats the bloke in black. "I was passing by and thought I would drop in to give you a quick once-over."

The bloke in black waits. He hears the Secretary and Mrs Mole gasping to each other, "He's a *School Inspector*!"

Then the voice of Mrs Mole returns. The voice is trembling.

"You are most welcome," she says. "May I ask if you were the inspector who gave the inspection when Mr Donkin was our True Head Teacher?"

"Oh no, madam," says the bloke in black. He

puffs out his chest further, for he is rapidly growing into this new role. "That must have been someone else. There are many of us nowadays, travelling the country, doing our duties. And perhaps it was long ago. We are now much more modern in our approach."

"More modern?"

The bloke in black ponders. Somehow, he suddenly knows what a Master of Disguise should say in these circumstances.

"Yes, indeed, madam. These days we pass by, drop in, inspect, report and then move on. Unless, that is, we discover something to cause us to elongate our stay."

"*Elongate?* What kind of something might cause *that*?"

"Something out of the ordinary, madam. Something that is not quite right. Who am I speaking to, may I ask?"

"My name is Mrs Mole," says Mrs Mole. "I am the Acting Head Teacher."

The bloke in black writes something in his notebook.

"I should tell you," he tells her, "that I am

already taking notes. I am already beginning my inspection."

"*Already?*" says Mrs Mole.

"Indeed I am. And I am noting the amount of time it is taking you to open these gates and let me in. I hope, madam, that you are not trying to delay my once-over so as to hide whatever is not right."

"Oh no, sir!" gasps Mrs Mole. "We should never do such a thing, for we have nothing at all to hide." The gate buzzes and clicks. "Please come in, sir. We are happy to welcome you. Please make your inspection."

The bloke in black pushes the gate. It opens. He enters. He sighs.

"Just think," he tells himself. "When I was at school they said I'd come to nowt. If only my teachers could see me now!"

11

Mrs Mole holds the door open as the bloke in black enters the school. She tries to smile. Her whole body is trembling.

"Greetings, s-sir," she says. "W-welcome to St Mungo's. Samantha, some coffee and biscuits, please, for our Important Visitor."

"Yes, Mrs Mole," says Samantha. "And there may be some dinner left over – ham salad, perhaps, or custard and cake."

"Custard?" says the bloke.

"Yes," says Samantha. "And cake."

"Ch-chocolate cake, sir," adds Mrs Mole.

The bloke in black hesitates a moment, then raises his hand.

"No, madam!" he says. "An inspection is not the time for custard-like frivolities. Speed is of the essence. Take me to a class immediately or there'll be trouble!"

The Acting Head Teacher glances in fear at the School Secretary.

"Professor Smellie!" hisses Samantha Cludd. "He's with the G&Ts."

Mrs Mole sighs. Yes! There was no Professor here in Mr Donkin's time, and hardly any G&Ts.

"F-follow me, sir," she says. "Our P-P-Professor will be delighted to see you. How shall I introduce you?"

"Be brief. Say, 'Here is the School Inspector about to give you his once-over.'"

The Acting Head Teacher pauses. She leans a little closer to the bloke.

"You seem v-very young," she says, "to be a School Inspector, sir."

The bloke in black twists the ends of his moustache. He raises his head and adopts a very serious expression.

"I am," he replies, "much older than I appear to be."

Be brave, she tells herself.

"Have I s-seen you before?" she asks.

"No, madam, you have not saw me before."

"Were you once a little boy called K-Kevin?"

"Kevin? Do I look like I was once a little boy called Kevin? And is this any way to address a School

Inspector? My name is Black, madam. Mr Black."

"And your f-first name, if I may enquire?"

"Bruno," says the bloke. He blinks, astonished that such a name has fallen from his lips. "Yes, I am Mr Bruno Black, the Chief Inspector of Schools."

"*Chief* Inspector!" gasps Mrs Mole in terror.

"Yes, indeed." He stands taller. His voice becomes even deeper. Yes, this truly is how a Master of Disguise should behave. "My promotion was confirmed today. Now stop delaying the inspection. Open the door and let me in."

She opens the classroom door and steps aside, and Mr Bruno Black walks in.

"The colon!" sighs Professor Smellie. His eyes are closed, his head is tilted towards the ceiling, the fingers of his left hand rest on his furrowed brow. "Then the semi-colon!" he continues. "The differences between them are so infinitely subtle, and yet so exquisitely precise."

The children, among them Alice Obi, turn their eyes towards the visitor.

"Consider the following sentence, for instance," says the Professor. "Listen for the timing of the pauses wrought by my colon and its brother the semi-colon. And as you listen, note the carefully chosen adjectives and the poetic effects of assonance and alliteration. 'I have three beloved pets: one is a sleek salamander; one is a panting pot-bellied pig; and one is a hungry horse.'"

"Have you indeed?" snaps Bruno Black. He opens his notebook and licks his pencil.

The Professor flinches and opens his eyes.

"This," says the Acting Head Teacher, "is the Ch-chief Inspector of Schools, Mr Bruno Black. This, Mr Black, is Professor S-Smellie."

"Ha!" says Bruno. "A Professor named Smellie who fraternizes with pigs and horses and that other thing."

"Salamander," says the Professor. "The smooth-skinned amphibian that is sometimes wrongly described as the newt."

Bruno scribbles.

"I was naming such beasts," explains the

Professor, "in order to communicate the beauty and flexibility of our tongue."

"You have a flexible tongue?"

The Professor frowns.

"Of course I do not, not in the way that the salamander does. And of course I do not in fact own such pets, Mr Black. I was using them simply as the subjects of my sentence."

"So you lie about your tongue, and you lie about your pets?"

"Lies? I should not call them lies."

"*You* may not call them lies, sir," says Bruno Black. "But I, the Chief Inspector of Schools, may do so. Oh yes, indeed I may, as may these little ones."

He turns to the children.

"Children, did this Professor tell you that he owned a newt, a pig and a horse, and indeed that this horse was hungry?"

"Yes, sir," answer Alice and several others.

"And did he then admit," continues Bruno Black, "that, in fact, he owned no such things?"

"Yes, sir," say Alice and several others.

"Yes, sir, indeed!" echoes Bruno Black. "You do indeed have a flexible tongue, my laddo! A flexible and slippery tongue which is leading these poor children astray. I make my first mark, sir, and it is a black one. Oh yes, a deep black mark from Chief Inspector Bruno Black!"

The Professor stares at him.

"*This,*" says Bruno Black, "could lead to deep, *deep* trouble."

"*Trouble?*" gasps the Professor.

"In fact, I wonder, sir," continues Bruno, "if you are a Professor at all, or if your whole presence at this school is built on fibs and lies. Indeed, I wonder if your ridiculous name is a fabrication, and if this is all some ridiculous disguise."

"Of course I am Professor Smellie! I am a Professor at the Grand and Ancient University of Blithering-on-the-Fen. I have seven Honorary Doctorates and I am a Fellow of—"

Bruno Black slaps his hands over his ears.

"Blah blah blah!" he says. "Your doctorates impress none of us here. Nor, in fact, does your hair."

"My *hair?*"

"Yes, indeed! You will have noticed that my own hair is carefully brushed, while yours looks like it has been in a howling gale. Smooth it down, man, straighten your tie and pull your trousers up! Show an example to these children!"

The Professor stares into the void. He does as he is told.

"Much better!" says the Chief Inspector. "Now, continue to teach. And watch your grammar."

"Grammar?" gasps the Professor.

"Are you suggesting, sir, that grammar does not matter?"

The Professor gapes. He tries to speak. Bruno scribbles in his book.

"Stop staring, Smellie," he says. "Continue to teach as I continue to inspect."

He sits at Alice Obi's table. He waves his hand at Mrs Mole, who is still standing at the door.

"You are dismissed, madam," he says. "I must be left alone now in my inspection of this lying messy-haired Professor."

She leaves and shuts the door. The Professor shuts his eyes again. He turns his face towards the ceiling.

Alice looks at Bruno Black.

"You don't really *look* like an Inspector," she whispers.

"What *do* I look like?" he whispers back.

"Marilyn Monroe? The Dalai Lama?"

He smiles to himself. They'd be good disguises to take on some day.

"Course I'm an Inspector," he says. "Now behave yourself!"

He scribbles important-looking notes in his notebook.

"The simplicity of the full stop," says the Professor in a loud but quivering voice, "is often to be desired. As is the comma, the…"

He hesitates, looks at the Inspector as if the Inspector is turning into a deep, dark hole.

"Continue!" commands Bruno Black.

The Professor hesitates again, then talks on. Bruno scribbles a drawing of a little angel in his notebook. He shows it to the lad named Paddy Armstrong who is sitting at his side.

"Have ye saw this thing, mate?" he hisses.

He slides fifty pence across the table. The lad's eyes widen.

"Aye," Paddy whispers.

"Where?" says Bruno Black.

"He's doing Art."

"Art who?"

"No," says Alice Obi, "Paddy means he's paint-ing with Ms Monteverdi."

"In the Art room," adds Paddy.

He takes the fifty pence and slips it into his pocket.

"The exclamation mark, for instance," says Professor Smellie. "As we have seen—"

"ENOUGH!" yells Chief Inspector Bruno Black. "These children – and I – have heard quite enough of this drivel! Don't you even know that it is *saw* not *seen*?" He waves his notebook in the air. "I have done with you, Smellie! You are leading these children astray. You are a hairy ungrammati-cal deceiver! Someone take me to the Acting Head Teacher now!"

Alice stands up.

"I'll take you, sir," she says.

What a very strange School Inspector this is, she thinks. And what a very strange school day this has become. But so much more interesting than G&T lessons with the Professor. It'll be good to get away.

She leads Bruno Black to the classroom door.

He pauses there. He turns to Smellie.

"I shall," he announces, "be recommending your immediate dismissal!"

12

Ms Monteverdi is always lovely, and today she's even lovelier than usual. The sun shines through the Art room window and onto her golden hair. She's in an orange top and purple jeans and dangly dolphin earrings.

Her class, including Jack and Nancy, are wearing art smocks. They're standing at easels with great big sheets of paper, jars of water, brushes, palettes of brilliant paint.

Angelino's sitting on an upturned paint pot on a table. His wings are wide open behind him. His dress is marked with the lunchtime mud. There's a little yellow custard stain on his chin.

Ms Monteverdi moves among the children.

"Wow, that's bloomin' gorgeous, lass!" she says, and, "That's comin' on just grand. How about a spot of red just there? And that line, look. Give it a bit more curve. Aye, *exactement* like that, me honey! Be bold and brave and believe that you can do it. Don't be scared to make a mess. Oh Ali, that is wonderful! Doreen Craig you have excelled yourself! Gadzooks, Mustapha, what a lovely thing!"

She claps her hands.

"How lucky I am to have this class!"

She squeezes past the easels and beams at Angelino.

"And how lucky we are to have you with us, lad!"

Angelino bows. He flutters his wings. He gives a little fart.

"Just imagine," says Ms Monteverdi, "if Leonardo had had this opportunity! Or Rubens! Or Picasso! What would they have given for…"

She turns to the door, for it has opened, and standing there are Bruno Black, Alice Obi and Mrs Mole.

"Visitors!" she calls. "Come in! Join in! I know you're a Very Busy and Important Woman, Mrs Mole, but get yourself an easel, pet, get some paints! Hello, lovely Alice! And who's this lovely fella at your side?"

"The Ch-chief Inspector of Schools," stammers Mrs Mole.

"It's grand to meet you, lad," says Ms Monteverdi. "Best way to inspect us is to join us. Come in. Get stuck in!"

"*What* would they give?" asks Bruno.

"They?" says Ms Monteverdi.

"Ruby, Picasso and the other one?"

"The other one was Leonardo, Chief Inspector. Leonardo da Vinci, who was perhaps the greatest artist of them all!"

"Yes. Him. What would he have given to have an angel?"

"Oh, my dear Chief Inspector. Such artists would give their hearts, their souls. They would give what these children give. Wide-eyed wonder, excitement, joy and gogglement."

She smiles.

"They would rip off their black, black suits and gaze at this creature through childlike eyes and recreate him with astonishment, charcoal, clay and paint."

The Chief Inspector watches her, the way the sunlight brightens her hair, the way her eyes shine, the way she smiles so easily, the way she—

"Come on, lad!" she says. "Get that jacket off. Relax."

He flinches, shakes his head.

"No!" he snaps. "This is not the time for taking jackets off, madam. Continue to teach! Are you still here, Mrs Mole?"

Mrs Mole scurries out of the room.

He sits down at a table. He watches Angelino. He starts his own drawing of the angel to show the Boss. Strange, the thing seems to be bigger than it was at lunchtime as it dived its way across the goal.

Alice sits close by and draws him, Bruno Black. Who *is* he? she wonders. He *cannot* be a School Inspector.

"Try a little shading there, Mr Black."

It's Nancy, standing at Bruno's side.

"Are you snooping, kid?" Bruno hisses.

She laughs.

"Of *course* I'm not. I'm trying to *help* you. Some shading there would show the shadow of the wings."

"I need no help."

"Me name's Nancy. We all need help. Mebbe you should have a closer look. Ms Monteverdi," she calls out, "I think the Chief Inspector needs a closer look."

"Indeed, *ma chère*!" says Ms Monteverdi. She flaps her arms. "Angelino! Could you flutter to the dear Chief Inspector?"

He does. He flies right over the heads of the laughing kids towards the Chief Inspector of Schools. He lands on Nancy's shoulder and sits there and looks into the eyes of Bruno Black.

"Aye-aye, kidder," he says in his nice light voice.

"This is the Very Important Chief Inspector," says Nancy.

Angelino grins. Ms Monteverdi comes to Nancy's side.

"Bet you've not seen nowt like him before," says the Art teacher.

"*Saw* not *seen*," mutters Bruno Black. "*Nothing* not *nowt*."

He scribbles in his book.

"Aren't you a lucky bloke," says Ms Monteverdi, "to meet such a creature on the day of your inspection?"

Angelino farts.

The Chief Inspector glares and scribbles in his book again.

"What are you writing?" asks Ms Monteverdi.

"Notes," says Bruno. "Details of the things what I have saw in here."

"Like what?"

"Like flying angels. Like kids which think it is OK to laugh at Chief Inspectors. Like teachers what don't know manners, nor grammar. Like things that lead to deep, deep trouble."

"Oh, Chief Inspector! Have a smile, pet. Have a laugh. We like a laugh here, don't we, children?"

"Yes, Ms Monteverdi!" call the children.

"The problem with poor Mr Donkin," says Ms Monteverdi, "was that he wouldn't have a laugh, a joke, a bit of carry-on." She lowers her voice. "It's the trouble with Mrs Mole, too…"

"That," declaims the Chief Inspector, "is because they are Important People with Important Jobs to do. Just as I, Bruno Black the Chief Inspector of Schools, have too. Enough of all this nonsense. Take away this silly angel. Continue to teach. I will continue with…"

Ms Monteverdi reaches out and strokes Bruno's brow.

"You've a few hairs out of place here, love."

She smooths them back into place. Bruno goes all dreamy for a moment, then snaps himself out of it.

"Enough!" he declares.

Ms Monteverdi goes back to her happy children. Angelino takes flight and goes back to his paint-pot plinth. Bruno starts the shading Nancy suggested. Then he stops, and quickly scribbles a note to himself:

NO! STOP WASTING TIME, KEVIN!

He crosses out KEVIN and replaces it with BRUNO BLACK.

PHONE THE BOSS! he scribbles.

He takes out his phone. He calls the Boss. The Boss answers.

"Good afternoon, Boss!" says Bruno in a very loud voice.

The teacher and the children turn to him in surprise.

"I am phoning the Boss," he tells them. "I am reporting my once-over to him direct. So you better be on your best behaviour. Better watch your grammar. There'd better be no more nonsense or you might be the next one for the chop!"

Ms Monteverdi laughs. So do the children. Angelino flutters into the air and they all gasp and paint and draw.

Bruno lowers his voice, covers his mouth as he speaks.

"Artists," he hisses. "We could sell him to an artist, Boss. They'd give anythin' to have a proper angel to paint."

"Good thinkin', K," says the Boss. "And I'm already talkin' to a vicar, a bishop, two priests and a football manager from Italy. They've not seen through you, then?"

"No, Boss. They suspect nothin', Boss. I'm a Chief Inspector of Schools now, Boss."

"Congratulations. You are indeed a Master of Disguise, K. Don't let him out of your sight."

"No, Boss. I'm lookin' at him right now, Boss." The classroom door opens. "Got to go, Boss. There's some custard just arrived."

And it has. Betty's coming through the door with a tray of chocolate cake and a jug of custard left over from dinner. She often brings extras to lovely Ms Monteverdi's Art room for the children. And there's a special delight for her today, of course, because Angelino will be there. She's beaming brightly as she enters.

"Chocolate cake and custard!" she announces.

Then she stops. She looks at the School Inspector. Her smile grows even wider and even brighter.

"Hello, Kevin!" she cries. "Why aren't you at school?"

13

Next thing we know, Chief Inspector Bruno Black is out of the Art room door, down the corridor, out of the school front door and running full pelt across the yard towards the gates with Mrs Mole and Samantha Cludd in hot pursuit. They can't catch up. Bruno's legs are long and fast. But when he reaches the gates he finds they're locked, so up he climbs over the fence, and down he jumps to the

other side and off he goes across the road until he disappears. Ms Monteverdi and the Art class watch it all from the window. Angelino flutters above their heads and squeaks with the excitement of it all. The kids urge Mrs Mole to run faster, faster, faster!

"*Caramba!*" calls Jack Fox. "*Fantástico!* Lift them knees up, Mrs Mole!"

Alice Obi grins.

"I *knew* it," she says.

Mrs Mole and Samantha Cludd lose sight of Bruno Black.

Back they dash towards the school.

Betty hurries out to meet them.

"Ee," she says to the Acting Head Teacher, "what on earth was Kevin Hawkins doing here?"

Mrs Mole slaps her forehead.

"Yes!" she says. "Hawkins! I knew I'd seen him before!"

"But what was he doing *here*?" says Betty.

She counts on her fingers.

"I'm sure he should still be at school."

"At *school*?" snaps Mrs Mole. "He said he was a School *Inspector*. He said he was the *Chief* Inspector!"

"Well, he's done very well for himself," says Betty.

"But he wasn't an Inspector," says Samantha. "He was an Impostor. And he said his name was Bruno Black."

"Why on earth would he do *that*?" Betty shakes her head. "Ee, he was such a canny bairn."

"A *canny bairn*?" says Mrs Mole. "Right from the start I knew that boy would come to no good! Samantha, call the police! Tell them A Monster Is On the Loose."

14

When Betty and Angelino get home after school, Betty starts making Bert's favourite: shepherd's pie with carrots and cabbage and lots of gravy. It's not the kind of food for Angelino, so she makes him a little bowl of raspberry jelly with banana yogurt and three midget gems on top.

It's dark when Bert comes through the door, and the stars are starting to shine.

Bert kisses Betty. He pats Angelino's little head.

"I went for a pint with Sam," he says.

"That's nice," says Betty.

"I told him about our Angelino."

"What did he say?"

"He said he sounded nice. He said he'd like to meet him. He said he was very happy for us."

"That's nice. I've made your favourite, Bert. Can you smell it?"

"I can, pet. Can't wait to get stuck in."

They sit down to have their tea. Angelino sits on

a baked beans tin and holds his bowl on his lap. He dips the midget gems into the yogurt and licks the yogurt off and he hums a little bit.

"He's getting bigger," says Bert.

"I know," says Betty. "I'll have to make him some new clothes. That dress is like a miniskirt. And you'll never guess what we've got to tell you, Bert."

"What's that, then?"

She bites her lip and widens her eyes and says, "He's learning to talk, Bert!"

"Never in the world! What's he saying?"

"Go on, Angelino," prompts Betty. "Tell Bert what you say."

Angelino puts his midget gem down. He licks his lips. He takes a breath and he says, "I don't know nowt and I don't know who I am."

Bert is speechless.

"What do you think of *that*?" says Betty.

"It's amazing," says Bert. "Well done, son. I'm very proud of you."

Betty grins.

"Didn't I say he would be, Angelino?" she says.

Angelino looks pleased.

Bert shakes his head in wonder.

"Ms Monteverdi taught him that," says Betty. "And he's learning to write."

"Well, I never," says Bert. "What a clever lad!"

"And even *more*!" Betty tells him.

"What more *could* there be?" says Bert.

"Flying!" says Betty. "Angelino can *fly*!"

Bert laughs.

"Of course he can!" he says. "He's an angel. He must be able to fly. Go on then, little'n. Give us a whirl."

Betty flaps her arms to encourage him. Angelino flaps his wings, and up he rises over the table and over the shepherd's pie and the midget gems and the jelly. Down he comes again.

"Ee," says Betty. "Don't they grow up fast?"

Bert laughs and laughs.

"What a bloomin' wonder!" he says.

He gets stuck into his shepherd's pie. Angelino licks and nibbles and hums. Betty eats and eats and smiles. She gives Bert a bowl of jelly and yogurt for himself.

"Do you remember a lad called Kevin Hawkins?" she says.

"Can't say that I do."

"He was a bairn at St Michael's Infants when I worked there."

"Aye?"

"Aye. He's telling people he's a School Inspector."

"He's done well for himself."

"That's what I said. Seems he's not, though."

"No? Ah, well. So what clothes are you going to make for Angelino?"

"I thought mebbe some jeans. And one of those nice checky shirts the kids wear these days."

"That'd be nice. You'll put holes in, for his wings?"

"Aye. And I'll make some shoes out of those bits of leather in the drawer upstairs. Won't he look lovely?"

"He'll look champion," says Bert. He laughs. "Mind you, the rate he's growing, you'll soon be making him another set."

"I know," says Betty. "Kids, eh?"

She winks at Angelino.

"Aye-aye, kidder," he says.

When they've all finished they sit on the sofa and put the telly on. Angelino's on Betty's lap. It's the news, and straightaway there's Mrs Mole.

"It's Mrs Mole!" cries Betty. "Look, Angelino, there's the Acting Head Teacher!"

She's at the school gates in her green coat talking about the Impostor Bruno Black who deceived his way into school today. Samantha Cludd is at her side, wearing a clean headscarf and big earrings.

"It was a dastardly act!" says Mrs Mole. "The Fake Inspector needs to be caught!"

Then Professor Smellie appears. His hair is brushed very straight.

"I have never been so insulted in my life," he says. "He called me – and I can hardly utter the words – a hairy ungrammatical deceiver!"

"Ungrammatical?" says the reporter. "That's rather strong!"

"And," says the Professor, "he attempted to have me sacked! And indeed I *was* sacked!"

"*Sacked?*"

"Yes. By the Acting Head Teacher herself!"

"But quickly un-sacked," puts in Mrs Mole, "once the truth about the villain was known."

"And what *is* the truth?" asks the reporter.

"The truth, sir," says Mrs Mole, "is that the Fake Inspector Bruno Black once went by the name of Hawkins. Kevin Hawkins."

"And who saw through this fakery, Mrs Mole?"

"It was our School Cook, Mrs Betty Brown. She recognized the Monster from the very start."

"Eee!" says Betty. "She said Betty Brown! I'm on the telly!"

But then she shakes her head.

"That's just daft," she says. "Fancy calling a lad like Kevin a *monster*. There's monsters enough in the world without tarring daft lads with the same daft brush."

"You're right, pet," says Bert.

At that instant, there's a rapping at the door.

When Bert opens it, two huge and helmeted policemen are standing there.

15

"The name is Ground," says the largest policeman once they are inside and sitting massively on Bert and Betty's little sofa. He taps his helmet and points to the stripes on his sleeve. "*Sergeant* Ground. And my colleague here is PC Boyle."

The policemen remove their helmets and rest them on their knees. Boyle is very bald. He holds a notebook in his hand.

"We are here," says Sergeant Ground, "to talk about a certain Kevin..."

"Hawkins, Sarge," says Boyle.

"Indeed, Hawkins," says Ground. "What can you tell us about him, Mrs Brown?"

"Well," says Betty. Her voice is wobbling slightly. She finds it difficult to speak in the presence of two policemen.

"Would you like some jelly?" she asks.

"No thank you, madam. We would like some..."

"Clues," says Boyle.

"Exactly," says Ground. "You knew Kevin in the past, I believe."

"Yes, sir," says Betty. "In St Michael's Infants."

"And did he have the makings of a criminal back then?"

"Oh no, he was nice as ninepence."

"*Nice?*"

"Yes, sir. Daft as a brush sometimes, of course."

"Daft as a brush?"

"Easily led, sir. It got him into all kinds of bother."

The policemen both narrow their eyes.

"Bother?" says Boyle.

"Explain yourself, madam," says Ground.

"Well," says Betty. "If somebody said, 'Climb onto the school roof, Kevin,' he'd climb onto the school roof. If somebody said, 'Bring a bucket of frogs into school,' he'd bring a bucket of frogs into school."

"Doesn't sound nice as ninepence to *me*, madam," says Sergeant Ground.

He looks very stern.

"Are you noting this down, Boyle?"

"Yes, Sarge," says Boyle. "*Daft as a brush. Bucket of frogs.*"

PC Boyle finishes writing, then turns to the table and stares at Angelino. Angelino stares back.

"Aye-aye, kidder," says Angelino.

Boyle jumps. Ground stares at the angel for a moment too.

"Concentrate, Boyle! Do not be..."

"Distracted," says Boyle.

He blinks and continues to make notes.

"Tell us more," says Ground.

"He loved my toad in the hole," says Betty.

"He's not the only one," says Bert. "You've tasted nowt like my Betty's toad in the hole."

Ground sighs.

"We need facts, madam," he says. "Toad in the hole is not relevant. We need facts that will help us track down this monster. Have there been any previous instances of fakery and impostory and..."

"He was an angel once!" says Betty, suddenly remembering.

"An angel?"

"Yes. Not a real one, of course. Not like our Angelino."

"Angelino?"

"Yes, our angel. That's him on the table."

The two policemen slowly turn their heads to look again at Angelino. The angel leans against his baked beans tin, nibbles a midget gem and looks straight back at them.

"In the school Christmas play," continues Betty.

"He was swinging from the rafters over Jesus and Mary and Joseph. That's where they put him to keep him out of bother. Ee, I can see him now. Daft little Kevin flapping his wings!" She giggles. "And then down he falls – *crash bang wallop* – right into the crib!"

"Typical," mutters Boyle. "Little monster!"

"No damage done," Betty assures him. "Snapped wing, that's all. Course his parents weren't there to see him."

"Fed up with his daft-as-a-brush antics, no doubt," says Ground.

"Oh no," says Betty. "The mother would be swanning about with that fishmonger called Larry. And the father, well, he was always too fond of the Drunken Duck." She shakes her head. "Poor Kevin."

"*Poor* Kevin?"

"Yes, sir. After all, he'll still be hardly more than a bairn. What is he, fifteen, sixteen? Shouldn't he still be in school? Has he been thrown out?"

"It appears, madam," says Sergeant Ground, "that he has thrown himself out. It appears that he has not attended school these past six months.

It appears that he had *disappeared* from the face of the Earth."

Betty claps her hand across her mouth.

"From the face of the *Earth*?" she says.

"Yes, madam. And now we suspect that he has been hiding away in the criminal underworld until this moment, when he has re-emerged as a moustachioed Bloke in Black. He has become a Fake Chief Inspector of Schools. And now he has become..."

Sergeant Ground pauses, he takes a deep breath and then speaks in a Deep and Serious voice.

"He has become A Monster On the Run."

"A *monster*?"

"Yes. But he will not outrun the Long Arm of the Law. He will never outrun Ground and Boyle. He will... Have you anything else to tell us about him?"

Betty thinks.

"Well, he was a very good runner. He could spit further than any of the other boys. He loved dressing up in the school plays. He could imitate all the teachers' voices..."

"A veritable Master of Disguise," mutters Sergeant Ground.

"Yes, sir," agrees Betty. "And he could..."

"Could what?"

"Well, it's a bit embarrassing, sir."

"Spit it out, woman. We need the facts."

"He could break wind in tune, sir."

"He could *what* in *what*?"

"He could fart like he was playing a little trumpet, sir."

The Sergeant flinches.

"'Away in a Manger', sir. He could play that. And 'We Three Kings'. He was doing that just before he fell, in fact."

The Sergeant stares.

Boyle whistles 'We Three Kings'.

"That's how it goes, Sarge," he says to the Sergeant.

"I *know* that, Boyle!" says the Sergeant. "Are you writing this down?"

"Yes, sir," answers Boyle. *"Appears to have disappeared. Master of Disguise. Moustachioed. Bucket of frogs. Fart like a trumpet. 'We Three Kings'. Never outrun Ground and Boyle."*

Sergeant Ground stares into space. Perhaps he sees the same dark void that the Professor sees.

He lifts his helmet towards his head.

He pauses.

"May I ask," he says, "how you came into possession of this angel?"

"Oh, we don't possess him, sir," says Betty. "He just arrived."

"Arrived?"

"In me pocket," says Bert. "When I was driving the bus. I thought I was having a heart attack."

"And what are his intentions?"

"I don't think he has intentions, sir."

Huge Ground and Huge Boyle consider Little Angelino.

"He's very nice, isn't he?" says Betty.

"It seems," says Sergeant Ground, "that you think that many people and many things are very nice, Mrs Brown."

"I do," says Betty. "Because they are."

"*Are* they?" mutters PC Boyle.

He puts his helmet on.

Angelino farts.

The policemen stare at him.

"Bad Angelino!" says Bert.

"Can *he* play Christmas carols?" asks PC Boyle.

"I don't think so, sir," says Betty. "But we haven't known him long."

Sergeant Ground taps his cheek. He narrows his eyes and seems to ponder some great mystery.

"Farting angels. Moustachioed monsters. What is this world coming to?"

"Dunno, Sarge," says Boyle. "You're the Sarge, Sarge."

"Indeed I am," says Ground.

"I have some lovely treacle tarts," says Betty. "Are you sure you wouldn't like—"

"No, madam! Treacle tarts are not relevant!"

16

Once they've gone, Bert hums a few carols, then he has a snooze with the newspaper lying across his face. The Chancellor of the Exchequer is on the front page. He looks very stern. He says that people who are poor should be made poorer so that they will try much harder to become rich. His photo shivers and jumps about as Bert snores. Betty gets her sewing machine. She starts to make Angelino some jeans from an old blue curtain. She holds the material up against him to make sure they'll fit, and puts elastic around the waist so he can pull them on. She finds a checky tea towel to make his shirt. She cuts some holes in it for Angelino's wings. Angelino sits on his baked beans tin and sways and hums along to the sound of the sewing machine. Betty gets the iron and ironing board and irons the new clothes.

"Put them on, love," she says to Angelino. "Look, these go over your legs. This goes over your head. These holes are for your wings. You understand?"

He seems to. She turns around while he takes his dress off. She gives him a few moments.

"Ready?" she says.

She turns back. The jeans are on properly but he's all tangled up in the shirt. She helps him get it into place, easing the wings through the holes, then tugs everything down so it's neat. She brushes his golden hair with a little brush.

"Now stand up straight," she says, "and let me look at you."

He does. Betty puts her hands on her cheeks.

"Oh Angelino," she whispers. "Oh, what a boy!"

She taps Bert on the shoulder.

"Wake up, Bert," she says. "Wake up and have a look at our Angelino."

Bert pulls the paper off his face. He grunts. He rubs his eyes.

He can't speak. He puts his arm around Betty's shoulder. They gaze together at the little angel standing there on the table, all transformed.

"Aye-aye, kidder," says Angelino.

He farts. They giggle.

"Bad Angelino," says Bert. "Lovely bad Angelino."

They smile and smile and dab the tears from their happy eyes.

17

They watch a bit more telly but there's nothing on. Bert has a glass of beer. Betty has a cup of tea. Angelino seems delighted with his new clothes. He strides back and forth across the table with his head held high. He keeps smoothing down his jeans and shirt. Sometimes he jumps up and has a little fly around. A couple of times he stops and puffs out his chest and announces, "I don't know nowt."

Bert and Betty laugh.

"Yes you do," says Betty. "You know *lots* of things."

"You know your name," says Bert.

Angelino stares at him.

"Go on," says Bert. "Say it. My ... name ... is ... Angelino."

Angelino puffs out his chest and says in his nice soft voice:

My name is Angelino!

"Lovely!" says Betty. "Soon you'll be chattering away like all the other bairns."

Betty looks away and has a think. Then she leaves the room and comes back again, holding the photograph of the little boy from the bedroom wall. Bert sees it.

"Betty," he whispers. "Are you sure?"

"Yes, love," she says. "As long as you agree."

Bert shrugs. He gets up out of his chair and gives her a kiss.

"He's got to learn about his family, I suppose," he says.

"Angelino," says Betty. "Come and sit here a minute."

Angelino flutters from the table onto her lap.

Betty holds the photograph so he can see.

"This is Paul," she says softly.

Angelino looks at the face.

"He was our little boy," says Betty.

She looks at Angelino looking at Paul.

"Isn't he lovely?" she says.

"Lovely as you are, son," says Bert.

Betty sighs.

"He came a long time ago. But he couldn't stay.

He got very ill and very tired. He had to go back to Heaven."

Bert smiles and his eyes glaze over.

"Ee, he was daft as a brush sometimes."

Betty laughs.

"He was, Angelino. He could be a little *devil*, just like all you bairns."

"Paul," says Angelino softly.

"That's right!" says Betty. "Paul!"

"One of your family," says Bert.

Angelino leans close to the photograph so that his face is almost touching Paul's.

"Aye-aye, Paul," he says.

Then he dances around the table singing, "Paul! Paul! Paul!"

18

The evening passes by. Bert snoozes again underneath the Chancellor of the Exchequer. Betty makes Angelino some shoes from a piece of leather. She makes more clothes and he tries them on. A red shirt and a green shirt, a nice yellow-and-blue-checked jacket, another pair of jeans.

Then a pair of flowery pyjamas.

"Look at the time!" she says. "Where does it go? Put these on, son."

He puts the pyjamas on. He looks lovely. Betty licks the edge of the tea towel and rubs his face with it.

"Bert," says Betty.

Bert stirs and the Chancellor of the Exchequer flutters to the floor.

Bert rubs his eyes.

"Yes, pet?" he says.

"I think our Angelino should sleep upstairs tonight."

"You're right," says Bert. "He's getting far too big for that little box."

"Come along, then, little'n," says Betty. "Time for bed for bairns like you."

She lifts him up, gives him a kiss.

"You need to be bright-eyed and bushy-tailed for school tomorrow," she says.

"I've been thinking about that," says Bert.

"About what, pet?"

"I thought I might take him out on the bus tomorrow."

"Ee, but what about school?"

"He's got to see a bit of the world, hasn't he? And there's no better way to see the world than to sit in the cab with the driver of a bus."

"That's true. And I don't expect Mrs Mole or the Professor will miss him much."

"That's settled, then."

"And he'll see some of his pals on the bus, won't he?"

Bert nods and rubs his hands.

"What an adventure! Lovely!"

Betty carries Angelino upstairs. She lays him down in Paul's old bed. Angelino wriggles and twists and grins and is delighted to be there.

Bert puts the photo of Paul back on the wall.

They sit at the side of the bed and look down at little Angelino.

"We're very lucky, aren't we, Bert?" she says.

"Aye," Bert whispers.

"You should tell him a story, love. Like you used to."

"He won't even know what a story is."

"No, but he'll learn."

Bert ponders.

"I think I've forgotten them all," he says.

"No, you haven't. You never really forget."

"Don't you?"

"No. Once you start they'll all come flooding back."

Bert licks his lips. Angelino lies back on the pillow and looks up at him, as if he's waiting. Bert stares into space for a few minutes like he's looking at something far, far away. Then he blinks and turns his eyes to Angelino.

"Once upon a time," he says, "there was an old woodcarver named Geppetto..."

Angelino listens, and smiles, and sighs.

19

Next morning, Bert walks into the bus drivers' cabin at the bus depot. Lots of buses are lined up outside, waiting to be driven away. The drivers are drinking mugs of tea, reading the papers, grumbling about the chilly morning and moaning about passengers and bloomin' bus stops. Bert gets a mug of tea and sits down beside his mate, Sam. Sam and Bert have been driving buses since they were fine young fellas, a few decades ago now.

"I brought somebody to see you, mate," says Bert.

He lifts Angelino out of his rucksack and puts him on the table beside the great big teapot.

"This is Angelino," he says. "Say hello to Sam, son."

"Aye-aye, kidder," says Angelino.

"Hello, Angelino," says Sam.

He looks at Bert.

"You were right," he says. "Angelino's really nice."

"Course I was," says Bert.

The other drivers gather round.

"What *is* he?" says Bob Blenkinsop.

"He's an angel," says Bert. "Do a twirl, son. Show them your wings."

Angelino spins around and flaps his wings.

"Cool!" says young Lily Finnegan.

"Exquisite!" says handsome Raj Patel.

Angelino grins and farts and the drivers laugh.

"But how did he get *here*?" says Bob.

"I found him in me..." Bert begins.

"Now then, lads!" comes a booming voice.

"And lasses," says Lily Finnegan.

"Now then, lads and lasses! Gather round!"

It's Mr Oliver Crabb, Supervisor of the Drivers, coming through the cabin door. He has his Supervisor's helmet on. His jacket is tightly buttoned, his tie's neatly tied and his Supervisor's badge is polished bright.

"Listen up!" he says.

"The B136 is down to one lane at Pommery Cut and there's a major pothole on the A947 sliproad to the A2 and the Totem Viaduct has collapsed there's temporary lights outside the Drunken Duck and all the bus stops on the B333 have been moved a hundred yards and the High Street has been diverted onto the Low Street as there's a massive van outside Grimshaw's and there's still a roadblock between the A66 and the B45 and a flock of mad seagulls is dive-bombing the town hall and the black cat's on the prowl again on Black Cat Moor and don't forget your ticket machines and don't drive off until your doors are properly shut and why are the 326 and the X79 still standing

outside and why is the 92 blocking the 313 and why is the 124 pointing the wrong way and why hasn't the 42 had its overnight wash and why does the 75 say it's going to Slapton when it is supposed to go to Dipton and why…"

He catches sight of Angelino. His brow furrows.

"And why is there an angel in here?"

"He's with me," says Bert. "He's coming for a day out on the bus."

"Is he? Isn't there a rule about angels on buses?"

"I don't think so, Mr Crabb."

Mr Crabb takes a little book out of his pocket. He skims through the pages.

"It seems there isn't," he says. "OK, then. Off you go, lads."

"And lasses," says Lily.

"Off you go, then, lads and lasses."

"Angelino's nice," says Sam again as he and Bert set off for their buses.

"Aye," says Bert. "I know."

20

Today, Bert doesn't moan at all. He hums and sings as he goes along. He makes Angelino a seat belt from his rucksack strap, and the angel sits at Bert's shoulder on the top of the bus driver's seat.

Bert fell in love with buses when he was just a little lad. Today, he loves it all again. The way the engine roars and rattles and drums and purrs. The way the doors sigh open and shut, the way the gears click into place. He loves to turn the wheel and push the accelerator and press the brake. He loves to make the bus speed up and then slow down, to turn the corners, roar up hills and slide down slopes, to edge his way along busy streets and to cruise on country roads.

He laughs as he drives. He feels like the little lad he used to be.

"This is the life!" he says to Angelino. "The open road! Footloose and free! This is what it's all about!"

He points out the sights of the world to Angelino. The cars and lorries; the shops and pubs and banks and churches; the parks, fields, trees and hedges; the bridges, railways, rivers and hills. He tells Angelino about the sun and sky and drifting clouds. He tells him to look at all the people, the young and the old, the quick and the slow. Angelino giggles and grins. He hums some lovely tunes.

Bert smiles as he stops at bus stops.

"Good morning, dear," he says to old ladies with their sticks.

"Take care, mate," to old blokes with their limps.

"Let me help," to mums with buggies and bairns.

"No need to rush," to the kids on their way to school.

All of them see Angelino and all of them smile and sigh.

"Look," the mothers tell their children. "That's Bert Brown's little angel."

"So sweet," say sweet old ladies.

"So nice," say nice old blokes.

"Hello, little angel," say the little kids.

Angelino smiles and waves.

"We're very happy for you," say the happy people. They peer at Bert. "He's wrought quite a change in you, Bert Brown."

Indeed he has. All that morning, Bert drives and smiles and sings.

At lunchtime, he meets Sam at the Bus Driver's Drive-In Diner at the edge of town.

They have pasties and peas as they always do, and massive mugs of tea as they always do. Bert gets Angelino a banana with ice cream on top and the little angel smacks his lips as he eats.

"Nice?" says Bert.

"Very nice," says Angelino.

"It's not a bed of roses, of course," says Sam.

"What ain't, mate?"

"Bringing up bairns. Bringing up a lad like

Angelino. My lad was a handful."

"He'll be all right. Betty and me'll keep him on the straight and narrow."

"Course you will. But it's the commitment, mate. The money... How you going to keep him in pasties and ice cream once you're retired?"

"Mebbe I'll not retire yet."

"I thought you were fed up with it."

"I was. But then I remembered how it was back then. Remember? Driving the bus? Footloose and free?"

"Aye," says Sam. "It was all we ever wanted."

The men's eyes shine. They think back to their first school days, when they were little boys in the classroom of lovely Mrs Stubbs.

"Remember them little red double-deckers we had?" says Bert.

"And the bus garage we made out of boxes?" says Sam.

"And the trip buses we pretended to drive to Blackpool?"

"Aye, mate. Aye."

They laugh. Angelino watches them, as if he, too, can see them as little boys all those years ago.

They all look out of the window to the shining red buses that wait outside.

"Fares, please!" says Bert, in a little-boyish voice.

"Plenty seats upstairs!" says Sam.

"Vroom vroom!"

"Ding ding!"

"Ding ding!" repeats Angelino.

"Ha ha!" they all laugh. "Ha ha ha ha!"

They giggle. They eat their pasties and bananas and drink their tea.

The other people in the diner look across at them and smile.

But hang on. There's a white-haired bloke with a white beard all dressed in white peering at them over the top of his newspaper. It can't be. Can it? He looks so different, but...

Bert and Sam finish their lunch. They go back to their buses.

"Vroom vroom!" says Sam.

"Ding ding!" says Bert.

"Vroom vroom ding ding!" sings Angelino from Bert's shoulder.

The friends drive happily away.

The bloke in white watches it all from the diner window.

He takes out his phone.

"Yes, Boss," he whispers into it. "Definitely them, Boss."

"But you've let them out of your sight!" says the Boss.

"Don't worry, Boss. I know every bus stop on Bert Brown's route."

21

Bert drives back into town. Outside St Mungo's School there's a small bunch of kids at the bus stop.

Three of them, with Ms Monteverdi. It's Nancy, Jack and Alice Obi. They have notebooks and sketchbooks and pencils and pens. Alice has the old library book she had yesterday. Jack is in his Barcelona strip with the name of his hero printed on the back. Angelino dances inside his seat belt when he sees them getting on the bus.

"We're doing a project," says Nancy.

"A project?" says Bert.

"Yes. It's all about Buses and Angels."

"It's new," says Alice Obi. "It's experimental."

Ms Monteverdi laughs. "Will you allow this happy crew to create our project on your bus?"

"I will indeed," says Bert.

He knows how thrilled Betty will be to think he's part of an Experimental School Project.

"Champion," says Ms Monteverdi. "Me name's Millicent, by the way."

"Bert," says Bert.

She gives him the fares.

"To tell the truth," says Nancy, "I think Mrs Mole just wanted us out of the way. A Government Advisor's coming to school today."

"That sounds important," says Bert.

Nancy laughs.

"His name is Cornelius Nutt. Poor Mrs Mole is in a proper tizz about it."

She waves to Angelino. He waves back.

"Could we borrow Angelino for a little while?" she asks Bert.

"Borrow?" says Bert.

"We'd like to look at him," she says, "to draw him, to talk to him, to get to know him better."

"We're exploring the nature of angels," explains Alice Obi. "We'll ponder how angels are just like us, and how they are very different from us too."

She shows Bert her library book.

"There are pictures of angels in here but none of them are quite like our Angelino."

She shows Bert a couple – glorious white-and-golden things with glorious high wings.

Bert laughs.

"Ha! The folk that drew them have never seen a proper angel like our Angelino! Mebbe somebody should make a book with *him* inside."

"Yes!" says Alice. "We're the ones to do it, and we'll start it on this bus today!"

"Come on, Driver!" shouts somebody from the back of the bus. "There's places to go and people to see."

"Sorry, folks!" shouts Bert.

He releases Angelino from the seat belt and hands him into Nancy's care. He can't stop smiling. Who'd have thought that the dreams he'd dreamed in Mrs Stubbs' Reception Class would lead to something as marvellous as this?

They all sit down, and Bert drives on.

Jack switches on a little sound recorder.

They open their notebooks and sketchbooks.

Angelino sits on Nancy's knee.

"Speak into the microphone," she says to him, "so that we can record your voice. I love your new clothes, by the way!"

"Thank you," says Angelino.

"Who made them?" asks Nancy.

"Betty Brown!" says Angelino.

"And who drives the bus?" asks Jack Fox.

"Bert Brown," says Angelino.

They smile.

"Your speech is coming along so well," says Alice Obi. "And you're growing up so fast!"

Angelino gives a grin.

"How do you talk so well already and grow so quickly?" marvels Nancy.

"And how do you know how to *write*?" adds Alice.

"I don't know nowt," says Angelino.

They watch him and smile. He smiles back. He's silent and he flutters his wings.

"We all know how to do those things," says Alice Obi. "Perhaps he's the same as us."

Jack laughs.

"*Si!*" he says. "Just like us, but with wings."

Angelino hums a tune, something weird and lovely, something they've never heard before. He tilts his head back and shuts his eyes.

"What's that tune called?" says Nancy.

The angel stares at her. He doesn't know. The bus rolls onward, through the town, through the country. They hardly feel it moving, they hardly hear it roaring. They don't see Bert looking back at them through the driver's mirror. They're lost in their project, they're engrossed in little Angelino.

"Have you ever seen Lionel Messi?" says Jack.

"Have you ever met God?" says Alice Obi.

Angelino stares.

"My book says that angels are messengers from God," says Alice. "Have you brought a message? Have you come from Heaven?"

Angelino grins and stares. He farts.

"Where *did* you come from, Angelino?" says Nancy.

Angelino ponders very deeply.

"I don't know nowt," he says.

Gently, they all inspect his wings. The feathers are just like the feathers of birds, soft and downy ones overlaid with stronger longer ones. They're a speckled mingling of white, grey and brown. They grow out from his shoulder blades. He leans forward to let them see more closely. Sometimes he giggles softly, as if the human fingers are tickling him.

"They're so beautiful," says Nancy.

They all try hard to draw them, to give a proper impression of them, even though the bus rattles and sways and swerves. Ms Monteverdi says it doesn't matter about the wobbly lines caused by the bus.

"There's no such thing as perfect art!" she declares. "You're drawing and seeing and dreaming and imagining. Draw on! You're looking close, you're showing truth."

They inspect and draw Angelino's toes and fingers, which are just like tiny human ones.

"Have you got a heart?" says Nancy. "Just like we do?"

"I don't know nowt," says Angelino.

She lifts him up and listens to his chest, and despite the bus she hears it there, and she gasps and grins.

"*Bump bumpity bump,*" she says. "You *do*, Angelino!"

She takes his hand and presses it against his chest.

"Feel it!" she says. "*Bump bumpity bump.* Can you feel it, Angelino?"

Angelino's eyes widen and brighten.

"*Bump!*" he says. "*Bump bumpity bump!*"

The angel has a heart, they write. *The angel has fingers and toes, like us. The angel, in many ways, is just like us.*

"My mum used to say I was a little angel," says Nancy.

"Mine said I was a devil," laughs Jack.

137

"Some tales say that the Devil himself was once an angel," says Alice.

"How come?" asks Jack Fox.

"He lived in Heaven with God," Alice explains, "but he wouldn't do what God wanted so God threw him out. The Devil was a rebel against God."

Nancy writes down that little tale.

"Were you a rebel, Angelino?" she asks. "Did God throw you out of Heaven down to Earth?"

Angelino farts.

"I can't believe that anyone would ever throw *you* out, Angelino," says Millicent Monteverdi.

She touches his hair. So soft, just like a baby's.

They draw and write and talk and speculate as the bus meanders through the town, as it stops and starts, as passengers get on and get off again, as some of them nudge each other and say, "An angel! Look, a little angel!" Sometimes Bert grins at them through his bus driver's mirror. Once or twice he toots his horn. The bus rolls on, stopping and starting, sighing and groaning, rattling and humming.

Jack moves the sound recorder through the air, to catch the babble of voices, to catch the music of

the engine and the brakes and doors and of everyone inside the bus.

Outside, the sun is shining from above the rooftops.

"Aren't we lucky," says Ms Monteverdi, "to be
out in such a lovely world on such a lovely day!"

Angelino flaps his wings. He flies and hovers
over the children and they draw him flying there, so
light, so strange, so beautiful. He twists and turns.
The bus drives on. Its engine roars, its gears grind.
It slows, it stops. Its doors sigh open.

And a hand suddenly reaches up into the air and
grabs the little angel.

It's the bloke in white with the white beard! He's
been on the bus all along! He's got Angelino in his
fist! He dashes through the door and out into the
crowded streets and is lost from sight.

22

Imagine this. A small white room with a single light bulb hanging from the ceiling. A single window with black curtains pulled across it. A square table in the middle of the room. Two chairs face each other. A white-bearded bloke dressed in white sits in one of them. Yes, it's him, the bloke from the bus. It's Bruno Black, the Chief Inspector of Schools. It's Kevin Hawkins, Master of Disguise. He's sitting opposite another bloke. This one's dressed in black with a black cowboy mask covering his eyes. It must be the Boss. Lying across the table is a steel chain. One end is nailed down, the other is fastened to the ankle of an angel wearing jeans and a checky shirt with holes in the shoulders for his wings. Angelino.

The angel sits with his face in his hands and his elbows on his knees.

The Boss grins.

"Well done, K," he says.

"Thanks, Boss."

"You're a Proper Villain now."

"Thanks, Boss."

The Boss leans forward and stares down at Angelino.

"You've had it easy up to now, lad," he snarls. "Bus drivers' pockets and nice school dinners and lovely sweet bairns and everybody saying, 'Oh, isn't he lovely,' and "Look how he flies,' and 'Listen to how he speaks,' and 'Isn't he just the loveliest little angel we've ever seen in our lovely, lovely world?' Well, welcome to the real world, sonny. Welcome to the world of the Boss and his sidekick, K. We are Wicked, we are Evil. We are Monsters. We are your worst *Nightmare*!"

The Boss lowers his face closer to the little angel.

"We," he whispers, "are the Devil."

The two blokes laugh a wicked laugh.

"I want Bert," says Angelino. "I want Betty."

The Boss sneers. He laughs again.

"That's all over now, lad. You belong to *us*! K, the phone!"

K lifts the phone receiver, passes it to the Boss. The Boss dials a number.

"We got it," he snarls down the phone. "Aye, just like I telt you. Little thing with wings like birds... Aye, we'll be considering offers over the weekend. Starting price, a hundred grand... Credit? No, we don't take bloomin' credit. Cash or nowt. Get your bid in or you'll have no chance."

He clicks it off, clicks it on again, dials another number.

"Good afternoon, Your Lordship... Yes, we have indeed... No, sir, no one knows... Yes, sir. Of course, sir... Oh, he would look splendid against your gilded columns and your painted ceilings... I should say that there is interest from other quarters... Thank you very much, sir."

He puts the phone down, lifts it again, dials again.

"Badger," he snarls. "It's here... Now... Yes, the wings are proper real. No fakery, no tricks... Course he can fly... Course he'll look great in that massive bloomin' cage – they'll come from miles away... Food? Cake and custard, I believe. Not much more."

He puts the phone down, rubs his hands.

The phone rings. He lifts it up.

"Yes, Your Lordship. Of course we are in a position to sell. He is in our possession. No one else has any claim on him. He now belongs to us... No, sir, there will be no trouble from the authorities. The police will not become involved. After all, how can one steal an *angel*...? Thank you, sir... Yes, sir... No, sir... Certainly, sir... We will look forward to your bid, sir. Will it be possible to let us know by Monday?"

He puts the phone down, pokes Angelino in the ribs.

"This is the world you've come down to," he tells him. "A mad, bad, crazy rotten world filled with crooks and villains and with wicked blokes like K and me. And lucky us, we've just grabbed *you*!"

He giggles, snarls, claps his hands.

"You, my lad," he says, "are a bloomin' godsend!" Then he calms himself, and softly snarls, "So, are there any more where you come from?"

Angelino stares back at him.

"Any little feathered friends?" asks the Boss. "Any more of you turning up in bus drivers' pockets or dinner ladies' custard jugs?"

K laughs.

"Imagine that!" he says. "A little angel crawling out of Betty's custard!"

The Boss glares him.

"This ain't a laughing matter, K. If there's any other angels, we need to be the first to know."

"Aye, Boss. That's right, Boss. Sorry, Boss."

"You've done good so far, K. Beady eyes and good disguise. I'm proud of you. But you got to keep concentrating, you got to keep alert."

"Thanks, Boss. I do me best, Boss."

The Boss prods the angel again.

"Come on. Speak up. Tell us where your pals are. Tell us where they're hiding and flying. Is there any other pockets they've landed in?"

Angelino just stares.

"We have ways of making you talk," says the Boss.

"Have we, Boss?" says K.

"Course we have," says the Boss. "We've done them before, haven't we, K? Horrible things. Remember? Very, very scary things."

He glares at his partner in crime.

"Oh aye, Boss," K says. "Aye, I remember now. *Terrible* things."

"Good lad. Now keep an eye on him. I'm going to the bog."

The Boss steps out of the room.

"We haven't *really* done those things," K whispers to the angel.

"I want Betty," says Angelino.

K tries to sneer. The angel slumps. K reaches out and touches his wings. They remind him of the wings he wore in the school play, when he was in Miss O'Malley's class. They were made of strips of cardboard painted to look like feathers. He remembers farting "We Three Kings of Orient Are".

"I was an angel once," he says.

Angelino just stares back at him.

"Miss O'Malley used to say I was a little monster," says K.

"I want Bert," says Angelino.

"Don't think she meant it, though. She used to pat my head and say I just needed to concentrate a bit more. Like the Boss says now. Can *you* concentrate, Angelino?"

"I want Nancy," says Angelino.

K sighs. He shrugs.

"I know," he says. "But never mind." He thinks

I want Nancy.

about school again. "I was hopeless at sums but excellent at farting. Even Miss O'Malley used to smile when I did that. Would you like to hear—"

The phone rings. K jumps. He stares at it. It keeps on ringing.

"Get that phone!" yells the Boss from the bog.

K picks it up. There's silence on the other end.

"Hello?" says K.

There's heavy breathing.

"Where's the Boss?" snarls a deep voice.

"On the toilet," answers K.

He hears the toilet flush.

"He's finished," says K.

"Tell him Basher rang."

"Is there a message?"

The phone clicks and there's silence again.

The Boss hurries in.

"Who is it?"

"He's gone," says K.

"Who *was* it?"

"Basher."

The Boss stops dead still.

"Basher?"

"Yes, Boss."

"Basher Malone?"

"Dunno, Boss. Is there more than one?"

The Boss sits down. He licks his lips.

"Do you know him, Boss?"

The Boss stares into the void.

"I was at school with him," he says.

"Was he your pal?" says K.

The Boss's hand reaches across the table and touches the angel's wing.

"Was he nice?" says K.

The Boss just stares at him.

23

The man in white simply disappears from sight with the angel in his fist. The children and Ms Monteverdi jump out of the bus and run through the packed streets. Other passengers from the bus join in. They run through shops and supermarkets and cafes and pubs.

The children yell out, "Angelino! Angelino! Angelino!"

They stop passers-by.

"Did you see a man in white carrying an angel?" Nancy asks a sweet old lady pushing a tartan shopper-on-wheels.

"An *angel*? No, pet. Are you *sure*?"

"We've lost an angel!" Jack Fox says to a bloke in a suit and tie hurrying into a bank.

"An *angel*?" he answers.

"He's been *stolen, señor*!" Jack says.

"Are you having me on?" says the bloke. "Are you *mad*? And why're you talking foreign? And why aren't you at school?"

Everywhere it's the same.

An angel? Mebbe you got it wrong, pet. Mebbe it was a delusion, son – or an illusion. Mebbe it was a publicity stunt, a circus act, a magic trick. Mebbe you just dreamed it. Mebbe you should all calm down. Mebbe you should all just get back to school!

Bert drives back and forth through the town, down narrow shopping streets and round roundabouts and through estates and past great apartment blocks and supermarkets and pubs and restaurants and banks and churches, and nowhere is there an angel to be seen.

They all come together again in the market square.

Father Coogan from Connemara happens to be passing by.

He looks at them with gentle priestly eyes and asks what's going on.

"We've lost our angel, Father!" cries Ms Monteverdi.

He smiles kindly.

"Oh now, haven't we all?"

"We mean it, Father. We had an angel, Angelino, and now he's gone."

"It's *true*," says Alice Obi.

The priest recognizes her from his congregation.

He links his hands across his rotund belly.

"Now, Alice," he says, "haven't I said often enough that the images of angels in our church are simply that? Stone images. They are things for us to contemplate. Some say they are signs of our inner goodness, of our yearning for—"

Bert stamps his foot.

"He's a bloomin' *angel*! And he was in your bloomin' church just yesterday!"

"In my *church*?"

"Aye, with Betty."

"With Betty? I certainly saw your wife, Mr Brown, but I have to say there was no sign of any *angel*."

"Of course there wasn't! He was in her shopping bag!"

The priest blinks. He taps his cheek.

"I see," he says. "So the angel was in Betty's shopping bag—"

Bert stamps his foot again.

"Come on," he says. "Time to tell the police!"

And they turn from the priest and pile into the bus and off they go.

24

They dash in through the police station door. PC Boyle is at the counter with his helmet on. Sergeant Ground can be seen in the office behind.

The bus stands right outside.

"We've come to report a kidnapping," gasps Ms Monteverdi.

"We need your best officers now!" snaps Bert.

Boyle raises his eyes.

"Mr Brown. We meet again."

"Aye," says Bert. "And we need action fast!"

Sergeant Ground slowly rises from his desk. He comes through from the office.

"What appears to be the problem, Mr Brown?"

"Angelino's gone, Sergeant."

"Angelino?"

"The *angel*!" cries Nancy.

Boyle taps his notebook.

"The Angel Angelino, Sarge," he says. "Encountered on the same day as the Monster Hawkins."

"Ah, yes," says Ground. "And where has he gone, Mr Brown?"

"He's just gone! He's been kidnapped. Stolen."

"There's been an awful crime," says Ms Monteverdi.

"Somebody grabbed him on the bus," says Nancy.

"Somebody?" asks Ground.

"Somebody with a white beard dressed all in white."

"Are you getting this down, PC Boyle?" asks Ground.

"Yes, Sarge. *Angel. Kidnapped. Stolen. Bus. Beard. White. Awful Crime.*"

Ground nods slowly and sagely. He ponders the void for a moment.

"I'm a Police Sergeant, Mr Brown. I don't know about angels, Mr Brown."

"But you saw him with your own *eyes*," says Bert. "Last night. He was on the table eating midget gems and farting."

Ground ponders once again.

"Perhaps I did."

"*Perhaps?*" gasps Bert. "It's written down in PC Boyle's book!"

"Indeed. But we should not believe everything that is written down in books, Mr Brown."

"But look at these books!" says Alice. "We made them just today. Here he is! Angelino!"

The children open their sketchbooks. They show the drawings to the sergeant.

He laughs.

"Kids' books made by little kids!" he declares. "Start believing in things like that and we'll have to start believing in unicorns and dragons and tomfoolery all around us. What do you think, Boyle?"

"Dunno, Sarge. You're the Sarge, Sarge."

"Indeed I am. And my Sergeantly interest is in the criminal Hawkins. Not in an angel that is nothing but a distraction. An illusion, even."

"An *illusion*?" says Nancy.

"Yes, young miss. Illusions and tricks are everywhere."

"But he danced in my *hands*!" says Nancy.

"He saved my *penalty*!" says Jack.

"He let me *draw* him in all this detail!" says Alice.

"And we've *recorded* his voice!" says Ms Monteverdi.

"Yes," replies Sergeant Ground. He smiles sweetly. "Of *course* you have."

They all glare at him. He goes on smiling.

"Even if there *is* an angel," he says, "we must ask these questions. Can an angel be *stolen*, as an object can be? Can an angel be *kidnapped*, as a person can be? What do *you* think, PC Boyle?"

Boyle scratches his head.

"Leave that to you, Sarge. You're the Sarge, Sarge."

"Thank you, Boyle. Indeed I am the Sarge, and this Sarge knows of no laws that apply to angels. Write that down, Boyle."

"Yes, Sarge. *Unicorns. Tomfoolery. No laws for angels*. Very clever, that, Sarge, if I may say so."

"Thank you, Boyle."

"But they must be *connected*!" says Bert.

Ground raises his eyebrows.

"Hawkins must be involved in this crime," continues Bert.

"Aha," says Ground. "So now you are a detective, are you, Mr Brown? And no longer a bus driver. A rapid promotion, if I may say so."

Boyle sniggers as he scribbles.

Bert grinds his teeth.

"So do you believe, Detective Brown," says Sergeant Ground, "that it was Kevin Hawkins who … *took* the angel, Angelino?"

"Aye!" says Bert. "It must have been."

Ground nods sagely.

"PC Boyle," he says, "could you read me the notes you wrote yesterday relating to Hawkins's appearance and clothing in the school?"

"Certainly, Sarge," answers Boyle, leafing through his notebook. "Aha! Here it is. *Hawkins. Kevin. St Mungo's. Black hair. Moustachioed. Dressed all in black*."

"Thank you, Boyle. And now could you read your notes pertaining to the appearance and clothing of the snatcher of the angel?"

"Yes, Sarge. *Bloke. Dressed all in white.*"

"Thank you, Boyle. Anything else?"

"Beard. White."

The Sergeant smiles. Boyle sniggers.

"So, Detective Brown," says Sergeant Ground, "where is your connection *now*?"

Nancy marches right up to Sergeant Ground. She pokes him in the chest. He steps back in surprise.

"What are you *doing*, child?" he asks.

"I'm making sure you're really there," she says. "I'm not quite sure you are. I think *you're* the trick and the illusion. And I believe in Angelino more than I believe in *you*!"

25

The three children and their teacher pile back into the bus and Bert drives them all to school. They dash in through the front door. Bert jumps from his cab and runs straight for the kitchen.

"We have to see Mrs Mole!" says Nancy to Samantha Cludd, who is sitting in her office.

"She is in a Very Important Meeting," says Samantha, "with the Professor and the Government Advisor. They are planning—"

"But something *terrible* has happened!"

"I'm sure it can wait, dear."

"Angelino has *gone*!"

"That silly little wingy thing? Thank goodness for that."

Nancy decides to take matters into her own hands. She strides past Samantha Cludd and shoves open the door to Mrs Mole's office. Jack and Alice and Ms Monteverdi crowd in behind her.

"Angelino has *gone*!" Nancy yells to the

Acting Head Teacher and the Professor and the Government Advisor, that Very Important Man named Cornelius Nutt.

"Somebody grabbed him on the bus!" says Jack.

They all look up from their charts and their laptop screens.

"We searched and searched and couldn't find him!" says Alice.

"Ms M-Monteverdi!" exclaims Mrs Mole. "We are involved in Highly Important Educational M-Matters. Can you not keep these ch-children in—"

"But it's true!" gasps Ms Monteverdi. "One minute he's there, and the next he's gone."

The Government Advisor rises from his seat. He is very tall. He is wearing a grey suit and a white shirt and a very impressive striped tie and very, very shiny shoes. He peers down at the children and at lovely Ms Monteverdi.

"Of *whom*," he says in his Deep and Important voice, "are we speaking?"

"Of Angelino!" explains Nancy. "Of our angel. We were on Mr Brown's bus and—"

He raises his hand to silence her. He turns to Mrs Mole.

"On Mr Brown's *bus*?" he says. "What were these children doing on Mr Brown's bus?"

"It was an educational trip, sir. A project."

"And what was the subject of the project?"

Mrs Mole blinks. She licks her lips.

"The subject was Buses and Angels," says Ms Monteverdi. "It was new, it was…"

"Buses?" says the Government Advisor. "And Angels?"

"Yes, sir," whispers Mrs Mole.

"Is this how you intend to bring about School Improvement, madam? Is this how you intend to drag this school out of Special Measures? By getting these children to study *Buses and Angels*?"

"No, sir," whispers the Acting Head Teacher.

"But…" says Nancy.

"SILENCE!" booms the Government Advisor. "Professor Smellie, were you aware of this project?"

"I was indeed," says the Professor. "I informed the Acting Head Teacher that I would not demean myself by taking part in such a ludicrous farrago."

"Good man. You are destined for Great Things. Mrs Mole, see to it that the Professor receives a promotion immediately."

"Yes, sir," whispers Mrs Mole.

"Sir, we're wasting time!" says Nancy. "We need to rescue Angelino!"

"You are indeed wasting time," agrees the Government Advisor. "Any child not in a classroom is a child not learning. Time that is wasted can never be regained. You must return to your class. You must calm down and apply yourself to your lessons."

"But he's our responsibility!" says Nancy. "Angelino is a pupil at this school!"

"An *angel* is a *pupil* at this *school*?" The Advisor turns again to Mrs Mole.

"Oh no, sir," says Mrs Mole. "I can show you the r-registers, sir. He is—"

"But he was here yesterday," says Nancy. "He was flying in Ms Monteverdi's Art room. He was playing football. He was even in a lesson with the Professor himself."

"Can this be *true*?" the Advisor asks the Professor.

"I am afraid it is," says the Professor. "And I was wrong to demean myself in such a way. That creature was a source of chaos and confusion. He even helped to bring about my own dismissal, sir."

"But just for a little w-while," squeaks Mrs Mole. "Until we realized that the Chief Inspector was an im-impostor."

"An impostor?"

"Yes, sir. His real name is Hawkins, sir. He used to fart in tune. We chased him off the premises."

The Advisor blinks.

"And the Impostor Inspector Hawkins, named Bruno Black," says Jack Fox, "was the man in white who grabbed the angel on the bus!"

There's an eerie silence, disturbed only by the chatter of children in a classroom somewhere near by.

The Advisor Cornelius Nutt stares into the void.

Mrs Mole and the Professor stare into the void.

Nancy, Jack, Alice and Ms Monteverdi watch them.

"We're on our own," says Nancy. "It's up to us to find him and to save him."

They begin to back away.

"Perhaps," says the Professor suddenly, "we have all been the victims of some kind of mass delusion. A kind of hysteria."

"Yes!" says Mrs Mole. She clenches her fists. She tells herself to pull herself together. "That's it, sir. Hysteria brought on by the stress of School Inspections, of trying to emerge from Special Measures. The angel was not here at all. Nor was Hawkins. Perhaps this was what happened to poor Mr D-Donkin."

"Yes," says the Government Advisor. "Perhaps you should all get back to work. And perhaps we should continue our meeting another day."

"That would be best," agrees the Professor. "And it's Friday, so we have the weekend to recover, then we can start next week refreshed and renewed. Now I will go to Class 5P. I will deliver to them my lesson on the nature of the gerund and perils of the split infinitive. I will go right now."

But no one moves. The silence and the void return.

Then there is the sound of running footsteps in the corridor outside.

Bert in his uniform and Betty in her pinny appear at the door.

Betty's eyes are filled with tears.

The Government Advisor slumps and sighs.

"Who," he whispers, "are these people?"

"That's the School Cook," whispers Mrs Mole. "She gave the angel chocolate cake and custard. And that's the Bus Driver. He found the angel in his p-p-p-pocket."

26

"Torture!" says the Boss. "That's the way to get it out of you!"

Angelino stands on the table with his hands on his hips and the chain around his ankle and just looks back at him.

"Pain! Cruelty! Suffering! Tears! Confessions!" cries the Boss. He leans closer until his face is almost up against the little angel's own. "That's what's coming your way, sonny boy," he says.

Angelino shakes his head.

"What do you mean by that?" says the Boss.

"You're nice," says Angelino.

"*What?* You think I'm *nice*? Well, you've got another thought coming. I'm a Proper Villain, kidder, a Criminal Mastermind, a—"

"You're nice."

The Boss clenches his fist and waves it in the air above Angelino.

"No, I am not! I'm the Boss! I am *a Monster*. Ain't that right, K?"

"Yes, Boss," says K.

"See?" says the Boss. "Nice? HA! So you'd better watch out, laddo. Before we sell you on we're gonna get the *truth*!"

"The truth!" repeats Angelino.

"The proper truth. Who you are. Where you come from. Who your mates are!"

"I don't know nowt."

"We'll drag it out of you. Me and K! Won't we, K?"

"Yes, Boss," says K.

Now the Boss is waving both fists in the air and snarling and glaring at the angel.

"*This*," he yells, "is what I was born for!"

He laughs an evil laugh.

"Hahahahahahahaaaaa!"

"You look tired, Boss," says K. "It's been a long day, Boss."

The Boss calms down.

"You're right," he says. "And there's lots to do tomorrow, including *torturing angels*!"

He snarls at Angelino.

"I'll get some kip," he says to K. "You keep your beady eye on him. Any trouble, let him *have* it!"

"Yes, Boss," says K.

The Boss heads for the door. He grabs the handle, then he hesitates.

"Basher," he says. "He didn't leave a message?"

"No, Boss."

"Did he sound happy?"

"Couldn't really tell, Boss."

The Boss turns and looks at him.

"No," says K. "I don't think he sounded *very* happy, Boss."

"He never was. There was one time... But no, we don't want to remember that. Did he say where he was calling from?"

"No, Boss."

"Did he sound like he was near by?"

"Couldn't tell, Boss. Could have been in Australia. Could have been in the room next door."

"The room *next door*?"

"I'm sure he wasn't, Boss."

The Boss stares into the void for a few moments.

"I'll get a bit of shut-eye, should I?" he says quietly.

"Aye, Boss. Sweet dreams, Boss," says K.

"Night-night," says the Boss as he shuts the door.

"Night-night," says Angelino.

"Poor Boss," says K. "It ain't easy being Boss. So much to think about. So much responsibility. And he's just a lad, really, just like me."

He rubs his eyes and yawns.

"I'm knackered and all," he says. "It takes it out of you, getting the disguises on, inspecting, spying, catching buses, nicking angels."

Angelino sits with his legs crossed and watches K.

"We won't torture you," says K.

"No," says Angelino.

"Do angels get knackered?" says K.

No answer. K stares at him. He rubs his eyes again, then again.

"Are you real?" he asks Angelino.

No answer.

"Am I dreaming you?"

No answer.

"Mebbe I am," says K. "Mebbe it's all a dream. I used to think that when I was little. I used to think I was in the wrong dream, and there might be a better one I could go into."

He switches the light off and opens the curtains. There's a thin sickle moon high up in the sky and millions and millions of stars. Their light glitters like frost on the black rooftops of the city.

K points out into the universe.

"Is that where you come from, Angelino?"

Angelino lies on his front and rests his chin on his hands and looks up into the lovely night. His wings quiver above him. He says nothing.

"Do *you* think it's all a dream?" says K.

Angelino lifts his shoulders in a little shrug.

"I used to want to go out there," says K. "I had a little plastic spaceman called Sid. I made a rocket for him out of cardboard. I wrote his name on the side. I used to put Sid in the rocket and hold it up high and run round my bedroom pretending he was flying through space. *Zoom! Zoooooom!*"

K closes his eyes and remembers what fun it was and he sighs and softly laughs, and as he talks he really does seem to become younger, to become smaller, to turn back into the little boy he was.

"I used to make up stories," he says. "Me and Sid went flying billions of miles through the universe. We found lovely stars and lovely planets

and we lived there with a lovely family and lovely friends. They were aliens, but they were kind and friendly. Those stories were like dreams, but like dreams that were really real."

He sighs again.

"I tried to write one of the stories for school but the teacher just laughed." He imitates the voice of an exasperated teacher. *"Kevin Hawkins, you are such a messy boy! How can you expect me to make sense of something as messy as this?"*

He reaches down and gently touches the angel's wing.

"Dunno what happened to Sid and his rocket in the end. Probably me dad threw them out. He was always going on about me being a stupid useless baby and how I needed to grow *up* and toughen *up* and... Did *you* have a dad, Angelino?"

Angelino gives another little shrug.

"I loved me dad," says K. "And I loved me mam as well. I don't think they loved me very much. Me mam was always off with Larry the fishmonger and me dad was always in the Drunken Duck. Then they both cleared off and ... and I was on me own."

He stands and stares into the night sky. He remembers flying through the galaxies with Sid in the cardboard rocket. Angelino watches him, like he's waiting for him to go on.

"It doesn't matter now," says K. "I got put into care. I soon nicked off from that. Soon nicked off from school. I disappeared, Angelino. I've got a new life now. I got together with the Boss. We're a pair of Proper Villains. And I'm a Master of Disguise. And everything's better."

But he doesn't look like a Proper Villain. It doesn't look like everything's better. K looks like a Little Lost Boy. A little lost boy with tears glittering in his eyes who wants a cuddle from his mum.

Angelino hums a little tune.

"That's nice, Angelino," says K.

Angelino goes on humming softly and sweetly.

They rest together in the room and gaze into the beautiful immensity of space. Angelino hums and K joins in and together they make soft starry dreamy music.

"That's very nice," murmurs K.

"That's nice," says Angelino.

K starts to snooze and dream.

Angelino watches over him.

27

The same sickle moon and the same brilliant stars shine down on Bus Conductor's Lane. They shine into Bert and Betty's house. They shine through the window of Paul's bedroom and onto Betty and Bert, who are sitting together on the bed, holding hands. They've got down the photograph of Paul, and Angelino's cardboard box with his name written on it. They've got Angelino's little pyjamas and his clothes and their minds are filled with pain and they don't know what to do except to hold each other's hands and cry.

28

The night deepens. The moon and stars intensify. All across the city, the people in our story sleep and dream. Except the kids. They don't sleep or dream at all. They're wide awake. They're whispering to each other under their blankets on their mobile phones. They're planning tomorrow's search for Angelino. They're going to tell their parents that they're heading off together for a day in the park.

"We could ask Ms Monteverdi to help," says Nancy. "She understands. She knows it's a Matter of Life and Death."

"We can't," says Alice Obi. "She'd get the sack. Imagine the headlines: *Mad Art Teacher Helps Crazy Kids Look for Angels*."

"You're right," sighs Nancy. "They'd have her guts for garters. She'd never teach again."

"Who else is there?" says Alice.

"Bert and Betty?" suggests Jack.

"No," says Nancy. "They're both just too upset."

They all ponder. They know there's nobody. Nobody else would understand, or even *believe*.

"We're on our own," says Jack.

"On our own," says Alice.

They tremble in their beds.

"It'll be all right," says Jack. "If the Man in White was the Bloke in Black, he didn't really look dangerous at all. He looked just like—"

"A big daft lad!" says Nancy.

"That's right," says Alice Obi. "And we are—"

"A team!" says Jack Fox. He pats his Barcelona badge. "The greatest team! *El mejor equipo!*"

And in quiet voices, beneath their blankets, they make their plans.

THE NEWS

MAD ART TEACHER
HELPS CRAZY KIDS
LOOK FOR ANGELS

29

The Boss's dreams are deep, dark and disturbing. They're filled with ghosts and demons, monsters, witches. He tosses and turns, sweats and groans in his bed. His dreams begin to take the shape of Basher Malone, the awful massive bullying boy from junior school who scared the living daylights out of everyone. Basher's grown into a huge and scary hulk of a man. He's come into the room where the Boss is lying. He stands right over his bed. He gently taps the Boss's shoulder.

"Wake up, Boss," he growls. "Your old mate Basher Malone has come to call."

The Boss snorts in terror and wakes up. No one there.

Quaking and trembling, he goes back into the room next door. It is still night.

K's resting his head on his arms at the table. He stirs as the Boss comes in.

"I wasn't asleep, Boss," he grunts.

"It's OK, K," says the Boss. "No bother with the angel?" he asks. "No tricks? No escape attempts?"

"No, Boss," answers K.

"Good. Good lad. What you been up to, then?"

"Nothing much, Boss. Been looking at the stars and moon, Boss."

"That's nice. Mind if I join in?"

"Course not, Boss. You're the Boss, Boss."

The Boss sits down at the table opposite K, as he was before. He looks at the angel and then at K. He frowns.

"You look … a bit different," he says.

"Different?"

"Aye. Like younger or something."

K blushes. He doesn't know what the Boss is talking about.

The Boss shrugs, then looks out into the night.

"Stars," he says. "Lots of them, eh?"

"Aye, Boss," says K. "Millions of 'em."

"Billions," says the Boss.

He stares at the stars and the spaces between the stars and tries to imagine the stars beyond the stars that nobody can see.

He sighs.

"Where did they all *come* from, K?"

"Dunno, Boss."

"Me neither."

"You OK, Boss?"

"Aye. I had some funny dreams, that's all."

"I get them," says K.

"Do you? Dreams, eh? Where do *they* come from?"

"Dunno, Boss."

K and the Boss look at the stars, at the moon.

Angelino starts humming sweetly again. He flutters his wings in time with the tune. K and the Boss gaze at him.

"To be honest," says K, "sometimes I think I know next to nowt."

"Me too," whispers the Boss. "Absolutely nowt at all. Sometimes I just feel like..."

"A little bairn?" says K.

"Aye."

"What were you like, Boss, when you were a little bairn?"

The Boss thinks back. It wasn't long ago.

"I wanted to be hard," he says, "like me dad."

"And were you?"

"No. He said I was useless. He said I'd come to nowt…" He sniffs. "He cleared off when I was eight."

He sniffs again.

"Then I grew up and I thought, *I'll show him what I can do. I'll be the Boss!*"

"Does he know?"

"Not yet. I dunno where he is."

They sigh together. Angelino hums. They both lean down, and rest their heads on their arms. Soon they're breathing softly together, like pals, like brothers.

Angelino sits up straight and fiddles with the chain around his ankle. He slips it off. He stands and spreads his wings. He flies up from the table and hovers there, looking down at the Boss and K.

Then he hovers at the window, watching the dark shadows of the city below.

30

Out there, somewhere in the darkest shadows of the darkest alley beyond the darkest lane, a dark door opens. A dark figure steps into the night. A huge figure with thick shoulders and a thick neck and a thick skull. Thick arms, thick legs, thick chest. This figure moves in black silent soft-soled boots through ancient forgotten cobbled streets, over cracks and potholes, past shuttered hovels, half-demolished warehouses, ruined chapels, past doors that were last opened and windows that were last looked through a century or more ago. Rats scatter into holes in the earth as the figure approaches and passes by. Owls stop their hooting. Bats flicker to the safety of their roofs and steeples. Mice tremble, birds shiver in their nests. Even the light of the moon and the stars seems reluctant to touch this massive horrid moving thing.

The figure comes at last to newer places, to civilization, to where light shines down from street lights and out from closed shopfronts. There are voices here – distant laughter, someone singing high up behind closed curtains. A few cars, the night's late taxis, a single, brilliantly lit bus carrying passengers home again after lovely Friday evenings in pubs and restaurants and cinemas and theatres. A bunch of gleeful young people come into sight. They're chattering, singing, half dancing as they move along the street. They quieten when they see our dark figure approach. They drag each other quickly to the other side of the road. They turn and run. Did he even see them? Who knows? He moves on, relentless. He pauses only at one shop doorway. There's a couple of poor homeless folk in there, in thin sleeping bags on cardboard beds. He stares down at them. He snarls. He kicks them. He snorts as their eyes open, as they stare out of their troubled minds towards this beast who has come to call on them. He snarls again, he kicks again, moves on again. He turns his eyes upwards. He seeks the window behind which the Boss, K and Angelino are to be found.

Yes, this is him, Basher Malone. Somehow he knows about the coming of the angel. The image

of the angel now hovers
shining at the centre of
his dark, dark being. He
wants it for himself. He
wants Angelino.

And who could
save our little angel
from such a beast as
this?

31

Nancy hums as she swings back and forward on a blue plastic swing in the park. It creaks softly, in time with her movement. She's been coming to this swings park since she was a toddler, like all the kids round here. There's toddlers here already, with their mums and dads, their grandparents. They're laughing and yelling and squealing from the baby swings and the roundabouts, *Higher, higher! Faster, faster! Yeeeeeee!*

She swings higher, just like them. She loves to close her eyes until she starts to feel dizzy, to hear the squeak of the swing, to feel the breeze blowing on her face and in her hair.

And then here they are, Jack Fox and Alice Obi, coming through the gate. Alice has her library book. Jack has a rucksack on his back. They all give each other a quick hug. They're very bright-eyed and bushy-tailed considering they've been up plotting half the night.

They sit in a row on a green park bench.

Jack opens his rucksack.

"I brought some cheese sandwiches," he says. "And me mam's washing line in case we need to tie anybody up."

"Good thinking," says Nancy.

She takes some sheets of paper from her pocket and unfolds them. One of them is a very good likeness of Bruno Black. The other is a picture of the same face but with white hair and a white beard.

"We'll show them to people and ask if they've seen them," she says. "And this as well."

It's a beautiful picture of little Angelino in his jeans and checked shirt with his wings raised high behind him.

"We'll need it," she says. "'Cos when we say 'Have you seen an angel anywhere about?' they'll think of those perfect shining daft white things like in your book, Alice, not a proper angel like our Angelino."

"Good thinking," says Alice.

She takes a little foil-wrapped package from her coat pocket. She peels some of the foil back.

"Chocolate cake," she says. "So Angelino can

have one of his favourite things as soon as we get him back again."

"Brilliant!" says Nancy. "And we've all brought our great big hearts!"

"And," says Alice, "I've also found an experiment that might help."

"An experiment?" say Nancy and Jack.

"Yes. An Angel Experiment. I found it in this library book. It's weird, but it's worth a try."

32

They leave the swings park, away from the noise of the little kids and the roundabouts and the swings. Alice leads them into the shade of a great chestnut tree.

They sit together on the grass.

"I was looking through the book last night," says Alice, "and I came upon this chapter: 'How to Find the Angel'."

"Bloomin' heck!" says Nancy.

"Caramba!" says Jack Fox.

"First of all," says Alice, "you have to answer the question 'Do you believe in the angel?'"

Jack laughs.

"That's like asking if I believe in Lionel Messi! Of course I do!"

"Me too!" says Nancy.

"Good," says Alice. "Then you have to say if you are open to new and strange experiences."

Now Nancy laughs.

"After what's happened this week I think I can say we are!"

"Excellent," says Alice. "Now we all have to lie down."

The three of them lie with their heads close together, so that they make a star-like shape under the tree.

"Breathe deeply and slowly," says Alice. "Close your eyes. Be stiller and quieter than you've ever been before."

They try to do that. They hear the noise of traffic and people and leaves rustling in the breeze.

A young couple look towards them as they walk through the park, but they hurry on. All they see is three nice kids enjoying the shade on a sunny day. They see the motionless bodies, but not what's happening inside the minds, the hearts, the souls. Behind his closed eyes, Jack sees Lionel Messi skipping past defenders, curving the ball into the net. Nancy sees Angelino's hand reaching out from Bert Brown's pocket. Alice sees a library filled with shelves of wonderful books.

"Now," says Alice, "remember Angelino. Remember every little detail of his face, his body and his wings. Remember how he flies, how he dances, how – don't laugh – he farts. Try to think of nothing else. Imagine nothing else. Imagine him so clearly that it feels like he's part of you, like he's there inside you."

The three minds concentrate. Angelino takes shape inside their heads. He dances, giggles, farts and flies. They all stay very still. Nancy gasps, because she feels something like wings fluttering inside her chest. Alice sees something glowing beautifully in the darkness deep inside her. Jack hears a farted tune of 'We Three Kings'."

"Let him fly deeper, deeper, deeper," says Alice.

They all try to do this. Nancy trembles. She's never realized how huge she is inside, what massive spaces there are in her body and her mind. It's like she's moving through herself, flying through herself.

"In the book," says Alice, "it says we have to take Angelino as deep as we can, as close to the centre of ourselves as we can."

Jack laughs, even as he's feeling Angelino flying deeper, deeper. It's like when he imagines he is Messi, when he's running like Messi, when he's not just Jack any more but also Lionel Messi. Now he's Angelino, too, and he's also Nancy and Alice Obi.

"The book says you have to fly with the angel," says Alice. "Are you doing that?"

"Yes!" the others say.

"It's dead weird," adds Jack. "It's brilliant!"

They lie in silence, flying with the angel inside them.

"Then," says Alice, "when the angel is inside you, the book says the angel outside you will call out. That's how we'll find out where Angelino is."

They continue to lie and fly.

"Yes!" says Nancy suddenly. "He's calling!"

"Angelino is?" says Alice.

"Yes! I can feel him! I know he's somewhere near by!"

"Is he safe?" asks Jack. "Is he happy?"

"Yes!" cries Nancy. "No! I don't know. He's pulling me towards him!"

"That's what the book says should happen!" says Alice. "Where is he, Nancy?"

Nancy stands up. She turns through the shadow. It's as if there's a magnet working her, like she's some kind of compass.

"Which direction?" says Jack.

"I don't know," she says. "I don't think I know..."

And then, suddenly: "Yes. This way! Hurry!"

33

Basher's moving through the light now. The morning sunlight shines on him through the gaps between the city's buildings. His dark clothes are dusty, faded, worn. He's wearing shades – maybe because he's not used to so much light.

He lumbers forward in his big black soft-soled boots. He swings his head and sniffs the air. He hasn't done Alice's experiment, but it looks like he's being pulled by the same angelic force that pulls Nancy and her friends.

We don't know much about Basher, but I guess his name – is it his real name or a nickname? – tells us something. And the Boss's words about what he was like when he was at school tell us more. He was a big bullying boy, and as we saw when he kicked the homeless folk, he's a big bully still.

Look how folk swerve to avoid him as if he's a monster passing by.

Is he a monster?

Maybe he is.

Look how mums and dads hold their children's hands more tightly.

Listen to them tell the children to turn their eyes away.

Look how dogs cower from him.

A couple of times Basher snorts in a kind of laughter, but is it true laughter?

Yes, he looks very scary, but does he look very *free*? Can it really make him happy, to see people and beasts reacting like that? Could anybody *really* want to see such things? If we could see the eyes behind the shades and look into the mind behind the eyes, maybe we'd see something different.

Maybe, like lots of bullies and lots of nasty

blokes, he knows that something's missing from him, something that keeps him from feeling good, or even from feeling just OK.

Maybe that's why he wants Angelino.

Maybe he wants the angel to turn him into a better Basher, a better man.

Or maybe, if he gets his hands on the angel, he will do something truly wicked, something truly awful?

34

In the meantime, little Angelino's been hovering in the window over the Boss and K. He's been thinking about Betty and Bert, about Bert's pocket and Betty's custard, and about sleeping in the lovely bed that used to be Paul's and about his lovely new clothes and his lovely new friends.

And he finds himself crying, something that he's not yet done in his little life; something he's not yet done since turning up in Bert's pocket just a few short days ago at the start of our tale.

"I want Betty and Bert," he whispers to himself in a tiny, trembling voice. "I want my friends!"

A few tears fall from his eyes and run down his cheeks and splash down onto the table in the middle of the small bare room.

He looks out into the city and towards the hills beyond. It's so enormous, it seems as enormous as the universe itself. Where are they? Where are Betty and Bert and Bus Conductor's Lane and St Mungo's

School? Where are Nancy and his friends?

He seems to get smaller, to shrink.

"I want to go home," he weeps.

K and the Boss wake up.

They're amazed to see him up there in the air and the chain lying uselessly on the table.

The Boss gasps and rubs his eyes.

"You're free!" he says.

Angelino wipes his eyes.

"I'm free," he says.

He drops down to the table. He puffs out his chest.

"I want to go home," he says.

K sighs. You can see he really wants to do it, to give up this ridiculous farrago and take Angelino back to Betty and Bert and try to forget about the whole thing. And you can see that the Boss is tempted too. After what he said to K in the middle of the night, you know he's much less evil than he wants to be. But the day's come back and the Boss has remembered he wants to be hard, just like his dad. He wants to say to his dad, wherever he is, "I stole an angel and I sold it and I'm rich!"

He glares at Angelino. Angelino stares back.

His little face flushes. His
little fists clench. He gives
a little devilish growl. He
starts to become a different,
stronger, angrier, harder
kind of Angelino.

He spreads his wings
wide and he glares back.

"I'm *free*!" he snarls.

The Boss can't let an angel
speak to him like that. Quick as a
flash he grabs Angelino and wraps the
chain around his chest, and tightens it and
fastens it, and Angelino cries and the Boss
just laughs.

And the phone rings, and the Boss picks it up.

"Oh yes, Your Lordship," he says. "One hundred
and fifty thousand will make a very nice opening
bid."

He puts the phone down.

He laughs into Angelino's face.

"You're about to make us very rich," he says.
"Ain't that right, K?"

"Yes, Boss," whispers K.

"And no," snarls the Boss in his most Dreadful, Menacing and Evil-Sounding Voice. "You are not free."

Angelino weeps again.

He's small and scared again.

He's just a little angel, lost and all alone.

35

"I've lost him!" calls Nancy.

The children are on a street corner, between a florist's shop and a solicitor's office.

"What do you mean?" says Jack.

"I can't feel him any more!"

A nice old lady passes by.

Nancy shows her the pictures.

"Have you seen this man? Or this one?" she asks. "Or this little angel?"

"Can't say I have, pet," says the lady. "Though, to be honest, I sometimes can't remember me own name. It's Gladys, I think. Yes, it is! Oh, he's so lovely. I had a guardian angel when I was a bairn, you know, right here on me shoulder. What's your angel's name?"

"Angelino," says Nancy.

"Oh, what a lovely name! Mine was called Frank."

She moves on.

"Try," says Alice to Nancy. "Imagine him again, picture him again, start it all again."

Nancy tries, but she's too worried, she's too concerned, she can't be as still and silent as she needs to be. Alice opens the book. She reads the instructions again. She tells Nancy to imagine the angel right at the heart of herself, at the soul of herself. But Nancy can't. She just can't.

"Have you seen this man?" she says to a man hurrying past wearing a black suit. "Or this one?"

"What's it got to do with you?" says the man.

She shows the picture of the angel to another.

"Are you mental?" he says.

"Are you winding me up?" says a third.

"Kids!" says another. "What's gone wrong with kids today?"

"I can't feel *anything*!" says Nancy.

"Concentrate, Nancy," says Alice.

"Concentrate," says Jack. "Be silent and still. Be..."

Nancy sighs. She concentrates. Yes! Not as strong as before, but there it is, starting to turn her, starting to draw her...

Right then, a huge dark figure in black soft-soled

boots lumbers round the corner past the florist's shop.

Alice quickly turns to him.

"Have you seen an angel, sir?" she says.

"Yes," cries Nancy suddenly. "Yes! Come on! It's this way!"

36

Through twisted narrow streets they run. Across an estate of red-brick houses. Past shops and chapels, supermarkets, fishmongers and banks. Sometimes they hesitate as Nancy comes to a halt, closes her eyes, listens to the universe, searches inside herself. Then they hurry on again when she once more feels the angelic call. They come to an area of apartment blocks that stand high against the sky. Nancy knows that they're close now. She knows that Angelino's somewhere in a room above. She moves slowly now, footstep by footstep along the pale pavements, across bright grass verges, towards the shining glass doorway of a huge apartment block.

"This is the door," she whispers.

They hesitate.

"I'm scared," says Nancy.

"Me too," say the others.

Jack takes a deep breath. He touches his Barcelona badge. He knows what Lionel would do.

"Can't turn back now," he says. "Not when we're so close."

He takes out his washing line.

"OK," says Alice. "Ready?"

"Si!"

Nancy pushes open the door.

Their hearts are pounding as she leads them towards a lift.

They enter the lift.

Nancy reaches for the buttons on the wall.

"This is the floor," she whispers, and she presses the button for Floor 9.

The doors of the lift slide shut. As they do, the children catch a glimpse of the huge dark shadow that has followed them all the way. No time to think of that. The lift rises and stops. The doors sigh open. The children step out. The doors close again and the lift descends.

There are four doors facing them.

"This is the one," whispers Nancy.

It's Number 36.

"Be brave," says Jack. "All for one …"

"… and one for all," says Alice.

Nancy steps towards the door. She knocks. She knocks again. She knocks again.

No answer.

Alice knocks.

"Angelino!" Nancy calls. "Angelino!"

Silence from within.

Jack takes matters into his own hands.

"Stand aside," he says.

He rushes at the door, shoulder first. It doesn't budge. He kicks it with his orange football boots. It doesn't budge. He squats, opens the letter box, tries to see inside. Just darkness.

"I know I'm right," says Nancy. "I know he's in there."

"We know he's in there!" Jack yells. "Give us back our Angelino!"

No answer.

Their faces slump. What can they do? What are they? Just three nice harmless kids seeking their friend in a strange apartment block on the other side of town.

"Please!" beseeches Nancy.

Alice leafs through the pages of her book.

"Is there any magic in there for the opening of doors?" asks Jack.

"I don't know," says Alice. "I don't think so."

"Open sesame!" says Jack.

"Give him back!" yells Nancy.

And then the lift doors open once again, and here comes Basher Malone. He ignores the kids, pushes past them, strides on his soft-soled boots to the apartment door and kicks it down.

37

K and the Boss jump to their feet. They clench their fists. They grit their teeth. They get ready to face whatever it is that's coming for them. But they aren't ready at all. Now the door opens and they shudder, they shake, they're absolutely terrified. Here he is, the Boss's Nightmare.

Basher.

Basher Malone.

Huge and ugly, terrible and terrifying.

"B-B-Basher," whimpers the Boss. "Hello, B-B-B-Basher."

The Boss thinks he'll faint. He thinks he'll jump out of the window. He thinks he'll start crying for his mummy and daddy. But he just stands there stammering with his mouth opening and shutting like a petrified fish.

"Hello, Boss," grunts Basher.

He turns his horrible eyes to K.

"Hello, you," he grunts.

"H-help!" K squeaks in a tiny voice.

He clings to the Boss as he would to a big brother.

The kids crowd into the room behind Basher.

Basher takes no notice of them.

"What can we d-do for you, B-Basher?" stammers the Boss.

"Nothin'," grunts Basher.

He points at Angelino.

"This is what I come for."

He stands over the angel and stares down at him. Angelino stares back. Basher rocks on his soft-soled boots. He's never seen anything like this before. It's something he's been dreaming of ever since he was a tiny tot named Billy Malone. And he wants this thing. He wants it all for himself and for nobody else. It's his. He reaches down towards the angel.

"Don't you dare!" snaps Nancy.

Jack Fox gives Basher a great kick on the shin with his orange football boots, then another, then another.

Basher doesn't even seem to feel it. Jack gets his washing line and tries to wrap it around Basher's legs and arms but Basher just wrenches it away. He pulls it, snaps it.

"Begone, you horrible thing!" says Alice Obi.

Basher grabs Angelino by the waist.

"That's quite enough!" says Nancy in a voice like that of a stern teacher. "Put that little angel down!"

Jack punches and punches and kicks and kicks.

Alice searches through her book for ways to defeat monsters.

Basher unfastens the chain from Angelino's chest.

His eyes are shining, his mouth is drooling.

"Angel," he grunts in a horrible slobbery voice. "Lovely little yummy angel."

He lifts Angelino up. He inspects the wings with his horrible fingers and horrible eyes. He inspects the angel's bonny face. He lifts the angel to his mouth.

"Want you," he grunts.

He takes no notice of the hands of the children grabbing at his arms, his wrists, grabbing to save Angelino. He takes no notice of Jack's desperate kicks and punches.

"You're mine," he snarls.

He licks his lips.

He opens his horrible mouth, he shows his horrible teeth.

Angelino stares into the ugly face, into the ugly mouth.

"Angelino!" gasps Nancy. Tears are streaming down her face. "Oh, Angelino!"

But there's nothing they can do.

Basher Malone prepares to bite. His mouth gapes wider, wider, wider...

And then it happens.

Little Angelino spreads his wings. He grows suddenly bigger and stronger. He starts to redden, to turn the colour of fire and flame. He breaks free of Basher's grip. He rises into the air and, like a fiend, he glares down at the monster. He raises a fist as if about to strike him. He shows shining pointed teeth and brilliant burning eyes. He grows a red forked tail. He keeps growing, burning, growing, burning.

The children and the Boss and K retreat to the walls.

Angelino is a frightful, hovering, angry angel in the middle of the room.

His snarling is as vicious as his humming was sweet.

Basher tries to reach for him but it's no good.

He's starting to shake, to tremble.

Angelino hisses, spits, growls, snarls.

Basher tries to stand his ground.

He tries to glare back into the eyes of this transfigured angel.

But it's no good. Angelino's power is overwhelming Basher Malone. And Basher Malone is backing away. Basher Malone is terrified.

"Go away!" commands Angelino. "Go away!"

His wings spread wider, wider. He glows more brightly and more brightly and becomes more fierce and more fiery.

And, at last, the monster Basher turns away. He scuttles from the room and to the lift and to the ground and back into the city and back towards the dark and distant door from which he came.

38

There's silence left behind.

The children and K and the Boss stay where they are, back against the wall. They don't dare get close to Angelino. K and the Boss clutch each other. They goggle and whimper and shiver and shake. What will the angel do to *them*?

But Angelino has already started to shrink. His fire declines. His forked tail fades. He turns again into lovely little Angelino in his jeans and his checky shirt with his wings fluttering gently at his back.

He drops towards the table and he stands there.

"Caramba!" says Jack Fox.

The angel looks at them all as if he's never seen anything like them before.

He looks down at himself as if he's never seen anything like *himself* before.

"Angelino!" says Nancy. "I didn't know you could do anything like *that*."

Angelino shakes his head, purses his lips, wrinkles his brow.

"*Caramba!*" he whispers.

And he giggles. And he farts.

"Even angels," whispers Alice Obi, "have to be filled with fire sometimes."

The kids move closer.

"Are you OK?" says Nancy.

"Aye."

"Are you *sure*?"

"Aye."

"We thought we'd lost you," says Nancy.

"But we found you," says Jack Fox.

Alice points to the Boss and K.

"We found you with *them*," she says. "With this nasty pair of Kidnappers and Crooks."

Trembling there against the wall, K and the Boss don't look at all like Kidnappers and Crooks.

Nancy puts her hands on her hips. She glares at them.

"Who on earth do you think you *are*?" she says.

They can't speak.

Angelino spreads his wings. He glares.

K blushes.

"I'm K," he says.

"*K?*" says Nancy. "What kind of name is *that*? And why are you wearing that silly beard?"

"'Cos I'm a M-Master of Disguise."

"Ha! Master of Disguise! You're a phoney! Take off that silly ugly thing and tell us your proper name."

K winces as he peels the beard off his cheeks and chin.

"I'm K-Kevin," he says. "Kevin Hawkins."

"Ah yes. The Famous Monster Hawkins. Well, after what you've just seen, do you feel like a proper monster *now*?"

"N-no."

"N-no indeed! And *you*. You with the daft mask on. Who on earth are *you*?"

The Boss looks down.

"The B-B-Boss," he whispers.

Nancy takes a deep breath.

"First of all," she says, "take it off."

The Boss hesitates.

"Do it," says Nancy, "or I'll set this angel on you."

The Boss does as he's told. He lifts the cowboy

mask over his eyes and his head. He flinches as the elastic twangs and stings his ear.

"Now," says Nancy, "I will give you exactly three seconds to tell me your real name. One ... two..."

"Henry F-Falstone," he mutters.

"Speak *up*!"

"Henry Falstone."

"Aha! And what's wrong with the name Henry Falstone? It's a nice name. Why would you want to call yourself something silly like *the Boss*?"

"'Cos I'm a Villain," the Boss mutters.

"A Villain? Huh! Don't you think there are quite enough Proper Villains in this world without silly people like you pretending they can join them? Don't you think—"

At that moment, the phone rings.

Nancy picks it up.

"Yes?" she says.

She listens.

"Two hundred thousand pounds?" she says. "Two hundred thousand pounds for *what*?"

She listens. Her eyes fill with fire. She glares at Kevin and Henry.

"For an *angel*?" she snaps. "You think you can buy an angel for two hundred thousand pounds? ... Ah, I see, that is just your first bid, is it? And who am I speaking to? ... An *archbishop*? Then *I* am the Queen of Sheba! And I'm telling you I hope never to hear such claptrap again!"

She slams down the phone.

"You," she says in a sinister whisper to the Would-Be Villains, "were going to *sell* Angelino?"

"Yes," mutters Henry Falstone.

"Speak *up*!"

"Yes. We were."

The kids are aghast.

The very thought of such a thing is monstrous to them.

Angelino gives a little fart.

"Chocolate cake!" suggests Alice.

"Good idea," says Jack.

Angelino grins.

Alice takes the silver foil package from her pocket. She breaks the cake into little bits and passes it around. Not to K and the Boss, of course.

The last thing they deserve is chocolate cake. They still cling to each other in terror of the angel.

Alice gives the biggest piece to Angelino. His wings flutter fast.

"Lovely," he says.

They eat in silence, except for their little sighs of delight.

"Delicious," says Nancy.

She glares at the criminals.

"I bet you two feel pretty silly. You thought you were going to be rich and now you can't even have a piece of *cake*."

She continues to glare.

"*Do* you feel silly?" She stamps her foot. "Well, *do* you?"

"Yes," they answer at last.

"Good!"

Jack watches Nancy, wide-eyed.

"I didn't know you could be like *that*, Nancy," he says.

Nancy ponders deeply.

"Nor did I," she whispers. "But maybe children have to be filled with fire sometimes too."

"What shall we do with these two?" asks Alice.

Jack picks up the snapped pieces of his washing line.

"Tie them up!" he says. "Throw rotten tomatoes at them! Make them eat dog poo!"

Angelino giggles.

"Dog poo!" he repeats.

"Yes, dog poo!" says Jack. "Yuck!"

Then he picks at some crumbs of chocolate cake and licks them off his fingers. He shrugs. He knows they won't do anything like that.

"So what *can* we do?" he says.

He looks at Nancy.

They all ponder. What *should* they do with characters like these? What would the Acting Head Teacher do? What would the Professor do? What would Sergeant Ground do?

"Ms Monteverdi," says Alice, "would probably say that these two silly creatures were once two very nice little boys."

"Is Alice right?" says Nancy. "Were you once very nice?"

K shrugs. "I don't know," he says.

"Of course you don't *really* know. You were too young to remember. But you probably *were*. All boys when they begin are very nice indeed!"

"Like me!" laughs Jack. "I was once *very* nice!"

"And *still* are, Jack," says Nancy.

She smiles at him. Jack blushes. She blushes.

The phone rings. Nancy picks it up.

"Yes? Who am I speaking to? The Pope? The Chancellor of the Exchequer?"

She rolls her eyes.

"Oh, your name is Badger, is it?" she says. "Ah, you're a man of the circus, are you? ... Yes, the Boss is here but I am speaking on his behalf... Oh, you have a special cage, do you? And what do *you* think an angel is worth? ... Is that *all*, Mr Badger? ... Ah, you will go higher! Well, let me tell you, Mr Badger, you will go a good deal higher when I kick your silly bum. Now go away and find something *sensible* to do with your life."

She clicks off the phone.

"*What* a silly world you live in!" she says to the two impostors. "*I* think you should go back to the very start. You should go back to being little boys and start again."

"So do I," says Alice. "I think you should come to school with us on Monday and meet Ms Monteverdi."

"Excellent idea!" says Nancy. "Come on."

Kevin and Henry hesitate.

Angelino glares at them.

"OK," whispers Kevin.

"OK," says the Boss.

"OK," says Nancy. "Now, let's get out of this ridiculous place."

39

Back they all troop through the city streets, across an estate of red-brick houses, past shops and chapels, supermarkets, fishmongers and banks, through narrow streets and towards the city's bustling heart.

Angelino flies beside them.

Kevin and Henry trot unhappily behind.

"Come on," says Jack. "Let's *run*!"

They cross the park where they met up this morning. Jack skips and swerves on the grass as if he has a football at his feet, as if he's dribbling past invisible defenders. He laughs with the joy of it, with the joy of having Angelino back, with the joy of having escaped from Basher Malone. He lashes an imaginary ball into an imaginary net.

"Gooaaaaal!" he calls. "Yesssss!"

He punches the air.

Nancy and Alice cheer and applaud.

Angelino flutters and swoops through the brilliant sunlight.

Kevin and Henry just watch. Jack shows them his Barcelona badge, his football shirt, his Number 10.

"I'm Lionel Messi!" he tells them.

The pair look blank.

He groans.

"You don't even know who he *is*, do you?" he says.

They shrug. They sigh.

"Lionel Messi!" says Jack. "Lionel Andrés Messi! The greatest footballer the world has ever seen!"

"I don't know much about football," says Henry.

"Nor me," admits Kevin.

Jack is astounded.

"Don't know much about football! Did you never play it?"

"Sometimes," says Henry.

"Once or twice," says Kevin. "But not very well."

"*Sometimes?*" says Jack. "Once or *twice*? What have you been *doing* all your lives?"

He swerves and runs again. He scores, he leaps, he punches the air.

"You'll play on Monday!" he says. "You'll

play with us on the field and you'll understand!
Goaaaal!"

They hurry onwards.

"Where first?" asks Alice Obi.

"To Bert and Betty's house!" says Nancy.

"Yeeessss!" calls Angelino. "Yeeeeessss!"

40

Out of the park, along a few more streets, past the bus depot, and here they are at last, in Bus Conductor's Lane, at Bert and Betty's door.

All the curtains in the house are closed.

"Would you like to ring the bell, Angelino?" asks Nancy.

Angelino flutters, hovers, reaches out with his little hand and presses. No answer. He presses again. They all listen. Nothing. Then they hear slow footsteps in the hall. Angelino shivers, flutters, holds his breath. And then the door opens and Betty Brown peeps out, and she cannot believe what she sees there.

"Oh, Angelino!" she cries. "Bert! Just come and see who has come back to us! Oh, Angelino! Angelino! Welcome home!"

And the little angel flies into her arms.

41

Everyone crowds into the little house. They open the curtains and let in the light. They gather in the living room. Betty dances, holding Angelino in her arms. Bert stands and grins, and tears of joy are tumbling from his eyes.

Kevin and Henry linger in the half-lit hall.

Betty looks, and sees them there.

"Kevin Hawkins!" she says. "Were *you* involved in this?"

Kevin looks down at his feet and starts to cry like a frightened little boy.

"*Were* you?" says Betty.

"Yes," whispers Kevin. "I'm sorry, Mrs Brown."

"I am *shocked*!" she says. "I am ... *flabbergasted*!"

She looks at Bert; he is flabbergasted too.

"Tea," she says at last. "Tea and cakes and cheese-and-onion pasties and—"

"Midget gems!" says Angelino.

"Yes, midget gems and jelly, and you two silly people in the hall, come in here and sit on that sofa and don't get in anybody's way!"

So they all set to work. They lay the table with dishes of lovely food, with a jug of pop and a pot of tea. They sit down together and get stuck in, and they take no notice of the sofa-sitting pair until they have feasted together. Then the children tell Bert and Betty the tale of Angelino's rescue and of the horrors of Basher Malone.

"What a pair of *Villains* you two are," declares Betty.

"And what a trio of *Heroes* you three are," says Bert.

Betty wipes her lips with a napkin.

"Despite all that," she says, "I don't think they're truly *wicked*."

"They're certainly not truly *good*," snaps Bert.

"Maybe not," says Betty. "But who is?"

Bert smiles and takes her hand.

"*You* are, love," he whispers.

"Silly man."

They look at each other like a pair of young lovers for a moment. Angelino flutters over their heads. Nancy watches and imagines what a beautiful painting this would make.

"We think they've led each other astray," says Nancy. "We think they've been growing up all wrong. We thought we might take them to school on Monday."

"Nice idea," says Betty. "But what would Mrs Mole say? And the Professor? And the *Government Advisor*?"

"They'd probably say it was *ridiculous*," says Alice. "But I bet they won't even notice. They seem all bewitched and befuddled and bewildered by their Very Important Educational Meetings."

"And Ms Monteverdi would welcome them into her Art room with open arms," adds Nancy.

Betty sighs. She thinks of Angelino. She thinks of Paul. She thinks of how much love she has in her heart for them both. She whispers something to Bert. He blinks in surprise.

"Are you *sure*?" he whispers back.

"Yes, Bert. I am."

She sits up straight.

"I think," she says to Kevin and Henry, "that you both need a bit of mummying and daddying. Am I right?"

They say nothing.

"Is she *right*?" says Bert in a very stern voice.

"Yes," they mutter.

"Yes, indeed," says Betty. "So I think that the pair of you should stay here with us for the weekend."

The pair gasp. Are there tears in their eyes?

"But before *anything* else," says Betty, "it's about time you said sorry to this little angel."

They mutter something.

"Speak *up*!" orders Bert.

"Sorry, Angelino," say the pair.

"Say it like you *mean* it!"

"We're very, very, very sorry," say Kevin and Henry.

Angelino dances in the air and grins.

He gives a little fart.

"And," says Betty, "it's time to thank these fine

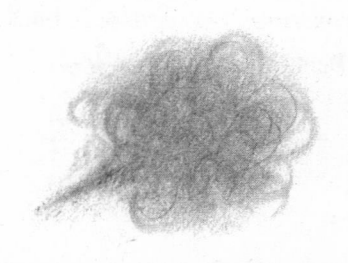

children for saving you from the monster and from your own silly selves."

"Thank you, children," say the imposters.

Bert glares at them.

"Thank you," they say again, and they really seem to mean it, they really, really do.

"Good!" says Betty. She folds her arms. "So! You two silly nitwits will stay here with us. You will both have baths and cocoa and an early night. Tomorrow you will tell us the stories of your lives. And then I'll take you into school on Monday morning with Angelino. Do you agree, Bert?"

"Yes, love," says Bert.

He folds his arms as well. He puts a very stern expression on his face.

"And if there's any bother from either one of you, you'll be in deep, deep *trouble*. Understand?"

"Yes, Bert," say Kevin and Henry together.

"Yes, Bert!" giggles Angelino. "Yes, Bert! Yes, Bert!"

And he gives a tuneful little fart.

"And mebbe," says Betty, "you'll turn out to be decent lads after all."

Time is passing. The day is rolling on.

Jack Fox puts another midget gem into his mouth.

"Me dad'll be wondering where I am," he says.

Nancy looks at her watch.

"And my mum," she says.

"And mine," agrees Alice Obi. "Time to go."

They all sigh. They don't move.

"What an amazing day," says Nancy.

"An amazing day in an amazing life," says Betty Brown.

She hugs them all.

"Go on, then," she says.

They hesitate. They hug her back. And then they go off to their homes.

42

So. St Mungo's School, on Monday morning. The Government Advisor Cornelius Nutt arrives in his big black shiny car. He makes his way through the knots of playing children. He is wearing his neat grey suit and his shiny black shoes and a very impressive striped tie. He has a briefcase in his hands, and a Very Serious and Important expression on his face.

A nervous Mrs Mole welcomes him at the school door. Professor Smellie is at her side. He, too, is wearing a grey suit and shiny black shoes and a neatly fastened tie. His hair has been very carefully brushed.

"Good morning, sir," says Mrs Mole.

"Good morning, madam," says Nutt. "I trust you slept well."

"Very well, thank you, sir," she replies. Though, to be honest, she looks as if she's spent a night in a room full of monsters.

"Excellent!"

The Professor clears his throat. He nudges Mrs Mole.

"I should inform you, sir," says Mrs Mole, "that I have promoted the Professor to D-Deputy Head Teacher."

"Excellent news!" responds the Advisor. He shakes the Professor's hand. "Congratulations, Smellie. The appointment of people like yourself into positions of authority will transform education in our country. Well done, Mrs Mole."

"Thank you, sir," whispers Mrs Mole.

She tries to smile, but instead she gasps. She shudders. She has just caught sight of an angel in jeans and a checked shirt flying above a football game at the far end of the yard.

The Acting Head Teacher tries to compose herself. She needs to guide these two men inside, quickly. Her knees knock, her voice wobbles.

"Please come this way," she whispers. "Ms Cludd has prepared a room for us and..."

She can't move. She can't believe it. Hawkins is out there too, running wildly about with the foot-ballers. It's him. She's certain of it.

"There will be coffee," she manages to say. "There will be—"

"Excellent!" says Nutt. "Lead on, madam."

She can't move.

"I do admire your suit, Smellie," says the Advisor to the Professor. "This is just what these half-wild children and their incompetent teachers need to see. They need something to look up to. Something to aspire to. Something to help lift them above the level of their narrow little lives."

The Professor blushes. He smiles.

"Mrs Mole?" says the Advisor.

She is staring out into the yard. It *is* Hawkins. He is bent over with his backside in the air. And the angel is—

"Mrs Mole!" says the Advisor again.

He sees what she is looking at.

"That boy," he says. "He seems rather older than the other pupils."

"Kevin has grown up quickly," she whispers.

"What on earth is he *doing*?" says the Professor.

"I think," whispers Mrs Mole, "that he is playing 'We Three Kings'."

The three of them stare out together through the

glass door. They see an angel fly above the bending boy. They see the angel bend over in mid-air and stick his bottom out, copying the boy. They hear the children below him roar with laughter.

Mrs Mole, Professor Smellie and Cornelius Nutt say nothing.

They are silent and still.

They stare together for long, long moments into the void, in which there are no laughing children, no farting Hawkinses, no angels.

Then Samantha Cludd calls them.

"This way, please," she says. "There is coffee inside, and biscuits, and a lovely leather chair for each of you."

They follow her obediently towards a door. There is a notice on it:

VERY IMPORTANT EDUCATIONAL
MEETING IN PROGRESS
DO NOT DISTURB
CHILDREN STAY AWAY

They step inside. It is good to leave the school yard and the void behind. Yes, it does look very clean and comfortable in here. There is a nice big desk and lovely soft leather chairs. There are pens and pencils and sheets of paper. There is a photograph of the Prime Minister and his wife on the wall, and another of the Queen. There is a photograph of the Secretary of State for Education, the rather handsome chap named Narcissus Spleen. The Advisor glances sideways at Spleen. Admiration and ambition stir within him. That is what *he*, Cornelius Nutt, aspires to be, the next Spleen, the very next Secretary of State for Education. And beyond that? He cannot restrain himself from looking at the picture of the Prime Minister himself...

"Make yourselves comfortable," says Samantha Cludd.

They do that. Smellie and Cornelius Nutt sit down proudly.

Poor Mrs Mole shivers as she takes her chair.

Samantha softly shuts the door behind them.

43

"A piece of cake!" says Ms Monteverdi. "Looks like they haven't seen you. And even if they have, they're so befuddled they can't believe it. This way to the Art room, folks!" She leads the children towards her classroom door.

Samantha Cludd stands in their way. She points at Kevin.

"Is that who I *think* it is?" she snaps.

"I have no idea *who* you think it is," says Ms Monteverdi. "I have no idea what you think about *anything* inside that very peculiar brain of yours. This young gentleman is, in fact, Kevin da Vinci, a well-known artist from the deep and sunlit South. Am I correct, Signor da Vinci?"

Kevin gasps. Nancy prods him.

"I thought you were a Master of Disguise!" she hisses.

"Zees ees correct!" blurts out Kevin. He's astonished at himself. He had no idea that he was about

239

to say such a thing until he heard it springing from his mouth. "And zees," he says, turning to Henry, "eez my colleague, Signor Henry Picasso. You may av heard of im?"

"No," says Samantha Cludd.

"Zat," says Kevin, "eez your misfortune. We ave been sent ere by the Grand Union of European Artists to paint zees angel inside zees school."

"What?" says Samantha. "That silly little wingy thing?"

"Oh, *signorina*," says Kevin, "you demean zees gorgeous and unique creature. You deed not know about zees?"

"I did *not*," states Samantha Cludd.

She stands her ground.

Henry Picasso steps forward.

"Signorina," he says softly, "as anyone told you zat you ave zee profile of a classical goddess?"

"Me?" says the School Secretary.

"Yes. You. You bring to mind zee work of Mozzarella and of—"

"Antipasto!" suggests da Vinci.

"Indeed!" agrees Picasso. "Zee great Antipasto. *Signorina*, I would love zee opportunity to paint you."

Samantha Cludd blinks.

"Me?" she whispers. "Me, Samantha Cludd?"

"Yes, *signorina. You!*"

Samantha's face softens.

"When?" she asks.

"Today, of course!" says Picasso. "Zat is, unless you ave anything more important to be doing."

Samantha looks towards the closed door of the Very Important Educational Meeting Room.

"Well..." she says. She ponders. "I will need to do my hair and put some make-up on..."

"Come just as you are," says Picasso. "You look wonderful already."

She blushes.

"OK," she says softly.

"Zees eez wonderful!" says Kevin da Vinci. "Ms Monteverdi, onward to zee Art room!"

And so they all go, with the angel dancing happily above their heads, into the sunlit classroom.

They put canvases onto easels. They spread great sheets of paper on the long tables. They find paints in tubes and in palettes and sticks of charcoal and pencils in all grades of hardness, and clay and plasticine, and they put aprons on and they sit

on tall stools and ancient wooden chairs and from the very start the large square room is a lovely blend of colour, of form, of dust dancing in brilliant shafts of light, of creatures called children and creatures called adults, and of a single creature called an angel who flies above and around them all and seems to fly within them all too.

The School Secretary is slowly softening, sighing, smiling as if she is becoming a different kind of Samantha Cludd. She sits upon a tall stool and Henry Picasso asks her to turn this way, to turn that, so the sunlight is like a halo around her face. And as he loses himself in watching her and in trying to recreate her with his paints, Henry gains in beauty too. As does everyone in the room, as they share the messy joy of making art.

Kevin Hawkins stares into a mirror. He paints himself, as he did years ago in lovely Miss Green's reception class. He paints a whole series of pictures that stretch back into the past. He paints himself

with white hair and a beard as the Villain, and in black as the Chief Inspector. He paints the unhappy silent boy in the unhappy silent home with the unhappy parents. He paints the yearning boy with the cardboard spaceship and the spaceman called Sid. He paints the farting angel spreading his wings over the stable and the nativity scene. He paints himself as a baby, sweet as all babies are, in his smiling mummy's arms. He paints these things quickly, and he lays them out to dry and then moves on to painting himself as he is now – just Kevin Hawkins, someone who looks half like a boy and half like a man, a boy who is growing up and coming to understand himself. As he looks and paints, he sees that he still has the image of the baby, the angel, the spaceman and the disguises still within him. He paints, and he is very pleased.

Many of the children create the angel. They model him in plasticine and clay. They picture him

in flight and at rest. They draw the detailed loveliness of his wings, the tiny fibres of the feathers. And Angelino performs for them, he rises and falls, tumbles and swerves, dances and soars. He comes to rest so that they can see him clearly, and then he rises again and soars again.

As they all work, Ms Monteverdi sings. It is something Italian and very beautiful. And she inspires, suggests, praises, corrects in her kind sweet voice. That's so luvly, petal. Ali, that is just *wunderbar*! A dab of yellow there, I think. Gadzooks, who thought you could do that! A stroke there like this, like that – oh yes, good lad. *Correctamundo!*

And soon other children begin to arrive, vagabonds from other classes, escapees from the G&Ts. They open the door, peep round, step in, mean just to stay for a moment or two to see the little angel, but under Ms Monteverdi's sweet encouragement they stay, they put on aprons, they get their can-

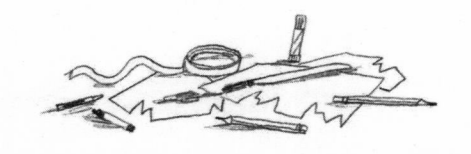

vases, paper, plasticine, clay, paints.

And teachers, too, are drawn towards the sunlit Art room. Maybe they have no class to teach, or they've come from curiosity, or they're searching for the escapees, but like the children they're drawn in and they stay. They create the angel, they create each other, they create the world that can be seen inside the room and through the windows, and they create other worlds from memory, from imagination. They make creatures with horns and wings, fairies and princesses and ghouls, aliens with five legs and seven eyes.

Ms Monteverdi continues to move, to sing, to praise.

"Paint with the brain," she whispers. "Draw with the soul, bring the image from your blood and bones."

They make images of professors and teachers and archbishops and crooks and priests. They make

images of the world's Basher Malones, coarse, half-formed dark and scary things. They make images of lovely creatures like themselves.

They create the universe – the unseen moon, the unseen stars, imagined other worlds and galaxies.

They fill the room with paintings, drawings, models. They hang them from the walls and from the ceiling. They place them on benches and shelves. And as the morning wears on, they create with more freedom, more passion, more delight. And the room starts to look just like a world itself, like this world, a world of loveliness and change and form and mess. A world that's packed with creatures, with finished things and half-formed things and hints of things, and with gaps and spaces where more, much more, can be imagined and created.

At break time some kids go out into the yard to run like wild young things, to visit the library, to gossip and natter, to play games of football. And then they come back to the Art room. It seems that on this weird morning the school timetable has fallen apart. No sign anywhere of Professors or Advisors or Acting Head Teachers. No teachers roar at the children and tell them where they must be but all are allowed to go into the room that is enlightened by the spirit of Ms Monteverdi and the angel, and by those children who saved Angelino, by those who stole Angelino but who have now seen the light. And sometimes in that room the children find themselves swaying, dancing, and as the sunlight pours across them and the glittering dust dances around them, it seems at moments that they almost fly.

Some time after break a shy and hesitant creature appears at the Art room door. It's the Acting Head Teacher, Mrs Mole.

Nancy sees her there. She and Alice Obi go over to her.

"Are you all right, Miss?" she asks.

"Yes," says Mrs Mole.

"Are you sure, Miss?" says Alice.

Mrs Mole looks into the eyes of the two concerned children.

"I slipped out of the meeting to go to the toilet," she explains. She pauses. "I don't think I want to go back again."

"That's OK, Miss," says Nancy.

"I don't think," Mrs Mole whispers very softly,

"that I want to be an Acting Head Teacher any more."

"That's OK, Miss," says Alice. "You don't have to be anything you don't want to be."

"You can come in here with us and with Angelino," says Nancy.

"Can I?"

"Of course you can. Let me get you an apron. Would you like to paint, to draw, to work with clay?"

"I don't know," says Mrs Mole. Then she stops and smiles and softens. "No. I do know. I think I would like to make some animals with clay. I did so love that when I was a little girl."

"I will get you some clay, Miss," says Nancy. "Come and sit here with me."

And so the Acting Head Teacher sets to work, a little tentatively at first, but Nancy and Alice encourage her.

"You can do it, Mrs Mole. You know you can."

And Mrs Mole smiles at her grubby, slippery fingers as they move about the lump of clay and begin to investigate it, to play with it, to mould and shape it, and she laughs with delight at the little cat that begins to come into existence between her hands.

Then Angelino is there in the air at her side.

"Aye-aye, lass," he says.

"Hello, Angelino," she says.

And he perches on her shoulder, and starts to sing a song, with words that nobody knows, but that everybody can tell are very beautiful and very kind.

44

The Government Advisor and the Professor are looking out of their window. They're looking across the yard to the Art room.

"Chaos," groans Smellie.

"Discord," sneers Nutt.

"A free-for-all. A mess. A—"

They hear the lunchtime bell. They can also see into the dining room from here. They watch the children and the staff pour in. They watch them dine. They see Betty Brown going from table to table with massive steaming jugs, pouring yellow liquid into bowls.

"Custard," says Smellie.

"And cake," says Nutt.

"See how excited it makes them?"

"Yes. Ugh! And look, is that Mrs Mole with them?"

"Watch how she lifts that custard to her lips. Watch how she licks it."

"Is that any way for an Acting Head Teacher to behave?"

"She is no better than the children."

"And look, there is that ... ugh! That ... thing on her shoulder."

They stare together at Angelino. They stare together into the void.

"No good can come of looking at such disturbing things," says Nutt at last.

"No, sir," says the Professor.

"Call me Cornelius," says Nutt.

"Thank you, Cornelius."

"And your name is...?"

"Cecil."

"Cecil Smellie. A splendid name for a professor."

"Thank you, Cornelius. It did cause trouble when I was younger, of course."

"Ah, I know all about that. Bullying?"

"Somewhat."

"We must all rise above such things."

"Indeed. And we are grown men, are we not?"

"Indeed. We shall bring order where there has been chaos."

"Where there is discord, we will bring harmony."

"Indeed."

"Indeed."

"Close the blinds, Cecil," says Cornelius Nutt. "It is best for men like us not to look upon such things."

"Yes, Cornelius. It will be better that way."

And so Cecil Smellie closes the blinds, and the sunlight leaves them and they continue their Important Work in the shadows.

45

The Government Advisor and the Professor are not the only ones in shade.

If we look beyond the school gates, across the road and on the other side of the little park, there's a deep black shape in the shadow of a dark building.

Can it be? Yes, it surely is! It's the monster, Basher Malone.

Strange, he doesn't look too scary as he stands there. See the way his shoulders droop, the way he hangs his head. He looks so sad. Can it be? A sad and lonely Basher Malone?

Of course it could be.

Maybe he'd love to join in with the art-making and custard-and-cake-eating. Maybe he'd love to be a friend of the angel rather than to gobble him up. Maybe he'd love to be little again, to be a schoolboy again. Maybe he'd...

Oh, look, he's turning away. Looks like he's heading back to the dark door in the dark street.

Strange. I feel a bit sorry for him. Do you? Maybe even Basher, a thing that seemed so ugly and horrible, could be turned into something good. Maybe there's a tale to tell about that. *The Salvation of Basher Malone.* That's a good title. Maybe an angel flies into Basher's pocket. Or maybe he finds one in his big soft-soled boot one morning.

Maybe anybody, even the Basher Malones of this world, could stumble across an angel and begin to change into a better person. Maybe he isn't quite ready to take part in Ms Monteverdi's Art class, or to drink Betty Brown's custard, but maybe one day...

Well, that's not part of this tale, but maybe you could tell it.

46

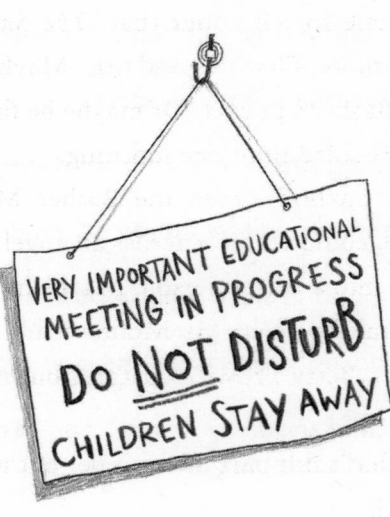

VERY IMPORTANT EDUCATIONAL
MEETING IN PROGRESS
DO <u>NOT</u> DISTURB
CHILDREN STAY AWAY

In the shadowed room, the meeting is almost done. How time has flown! Smellie and Nutt haven't even had the time to eat. But great decisions have been made.

"So," says Cornelius Nutt, "we shall present our decisions as a series of bullet points."

"Excellent idea," says Cecil Smellie.

"So, to recap..."

- Professor Smellie will become Head Teacher with immediate effect

- Mrs Mole will be sacked

- The school day will begin an hour earlier

- Art lessons will be chopped

- Morning break will be abolished

- Lunchtimes will be cut by 15 minutes

- Cake and custard will be banned

- Bus-based projects will be banned

- No child shall say "nowt" nor "aye" nor use a double negative

- All boys must wear suits and ties and shiny shoes

- Male teachers will wear ditto

- All girls must wear frocks and sensible sandals

- Female teachers will wear ditto

- All children will be tested in spelling, grammar, punctuation, multipl...

But we don't need the whole long boring list, do we? We all know the kind of decisions they would have made in their Very Important Long and Boring Meeting, don't we? So let's move on.

Smellie proudly holds the list in his hands.

"We have forgotten something, Cornelius!" he says suddenly.

"Have we, Cecil?"

"Angels, sir."

"Ah, yes, angels. Simple. Angels will be banned. Books containing references to angels will be removed from the library and from the classroom shelves forthwith."

"Excellent! I see why you are a Government Advisor, sir."

"Thank you. I will soon introduce you, Cecil Smellie, to Mr Narcissus Spleen. And perhaps you would like to have lunch with the Prime Minister's wife?"

"I would indeed, Cornelius."

The pair smile fondly at each other. They shake each other's hand.

"Shall we step out," says Cecil, "and share the outcome of our meeting?"

"Indeed we shall."

And so they do. But outside the room, things are strangely ordered, strangely quiet. Perhaps this is their perfect school.

The children, and everyone else, have gone.

47

This is what Smellie and Nutt missed while they muttered to each other in the shaded room...

Betty's pouring the last trickle of custard into a lovely lad's bowl. Angelino suddenly becomes excited. He squeaks with joy and flies to the dining-room window. A row of big red buses is pulling up outside, and driving the one at the very front, of course, is Mr Bertram Brown.

"It's Bert!" says Betty. "And look! It's Oliver Crabb, Supervisor of the Drivers."

It is indeed. Oliver Crabb is stepping out of his bus driver's cab and walking proudly to the gates wearing his beautifully ironed Supervisor's uniform and his splendid Supervisor's helmet. Behind him, in a happy little group, come the other drivers: Bert himself, Bert's best mate, Sam, Bob Blenkinsop, lovely Lily Finnegan and handsome Raj Patel.

Mrs Mole and Samantha Cludd stare at each other.

What should they do?

Mrs Mole wipes the clay from her hands and goes to the gate to greet them. Samantha follows.

"Greetings, madam," says Oliver Crabb. "I am Mr Oliver Crabb, Supervisor of the Drivers."

"And I am Mrs Mole, Acting Head Teacher."

"Splendid! I have come here with a gift for you all."

"A gift?" says Mrs Mole.

"Yes, indeed," says Oliver Crabb. "To celebrate the arrival of an angel in our town, the bus company has decided to donate an afternoon of free travel to this angel, and to everyone at St Mungo's School."

He beams.

"So," he says, "would you like to gather the children and follow these excellent drivers to their buses?"

"Just like that?" says Mrs Mole.

"Yes, madam. Just like that!"

Mrs Mole and Samantha Cludd stare at each other once again.

They find that Nancy, Jack, Alice and Ms Monteverdi are standing beside them. They find that Angelino is flying above their heads. They find themselves grinning, smiling, laughing.

"That'll be brilliant!" says Nancy.

"Thank you very much, Mr Crabb!" says Alice.

"You will find that there is cake and pop inside each bus," says Oliver Crabb, "to help with the spirit of merry-making."

"We could call it an Experimental School Project," suggests Ms Monteverdi.

"Yes," says Mrs Mole. "Buses and Angels and—"

"Children and Cooks and Drivers and—"

"Cake!" sings Angelino. "Cake!"

He flies to Bert and perches on his shoulder.

"Very well!" says Mrs Mole. She looks towards the window where the shades are tightly drawn. "But we must set off quietly," she says. "We don't want to disturb the Very Important Meeting, do we?"

And so it happens. Mrs Mole, Ms Monteverdi and Samantha Cludd collect all the children and the teachers and the assistants and the helpers and the cleaners from the dining hall, from the playground, from the classrooms and the library. They lead them out, tiptoeing silently past the meeting room, through the corridors, out of the front door, through the school gates and out to the waiting buses.

Soon the school is emptied and the lovely red buses are full, and there is just enough room for them all. Mr Crabb guides everyone to their places. Then he climbs into his own driver's cab, switches on his engine, gives the thumbs-up to Bert, Sam, Bob, Raj and Lily.

Bert Brown, in his lovely red bus, with the angel Angelino sitting on his shoulder and his good wife Betty sitting just behind, leads the happy procession away from school.

And all that afternoon they travel through the

city and through villages and towns and over green hills and past pale beaches and fields of dancing corn. And breezes blow and the sea shimmers and people wave and birds fly and dogs run and aeroplanes soar overhead. The world keeps on turning as it always has, and the sun follows its astonishing arc above us all as it always does. The buses carry people smudged with clay and spattered with paint, and they all eat cake and they all drink pop, and they all sing silly songs and happy songs, and Angelino watches and joins in and loves the fact that he turned up in a bus driver's pocket in such a lovely world as this.

48

The day comes to an end, as all days must. And this tale comes to an end, as all tales must.

The buses empty. Everyone goes home. Bert and Betty walk together from the bus depot to their nice little home in Bus Conductor's Lane.

Angelino holds their hands, and swings back and forth between them.

Betty laughs. "Angelino, you're becoming quite a weight, lad."

It's true. Angelino's a little taller, a little heavier than he was. What keeps him in the air is not his wings, but Bert and Betty's loving hands.

They all laugh.

Bert and Betty hold him tighter and swing him higher.

How he loves it.

"Higher!" he calls. "Higher! Higher! Higher!"

They swing him high.

"More!" he calls. "More, more, more!"

"Kids!" says Betty.

"Kids!" says Bert.

"Higher! Higher!"

At home, Angelino has a supper of bread and jam and midget gems. He drinks a little glass of milk. He stretches and yawns and his wings give a tired little flicker.

"Poor lad," says Betty. "You're all wore out."

They carry him up to bed and put on his pyjamas and lay him down in Paul's bed, below Paul's photo.

Betty and Bert sit on the bed.

Bert tells the tale of "The Little Mermaid".

Angelino sighs with happiness as he listens.

When the tale is done, Betty switches out the light.

"Night-night, son," they both whisper.

"Night-night," whispers Angelino. "Nighty-night."

That night they all sleep long and deep and dreamless sleeps.

The next morning, still in her dressing-gown, Betty goes in to wake Angelino.

"Come on, sleepyhead," she whispers.

He smiles at her through the morning light.

She lifts him up. She puts her arms around him. He's grown, yet again, and everything's different.

Betty looks down, over his shoulder. Angelino's wings are left behind. They lie there on the bed where he's been sleeping.

"Angelino!" she gasps. "Bert, come and see!"

Angelino giggles.

"Morning, Mum," he says. "Morning, Dad."

This all happened several years ago. Bert and Betty kept the wings, of course. They wrapped them in soft white paper and kept them in a nice clean wooden box. Sometimes they take the wings from the box, just to touch them gently and to look at them fondly, to remind themselves of how their Angelino used to be, before he turned into an ordinary little lovely boy.